SPOTLIGHT

JILLIAN JACOBS

JILLIANJACOBS.COM

Rolling Rocker news reporter shines the spotlight on Apollo band mates' Freddie Davis and TJ Hardwood. While interviewing Freddie for a piece on intimate partner violence, the reporter learns the two men really do make beautiful music together—both on and off the stage.

As childhood friends, TJ and Freddie Davis had a singular goal—to become rock stars. But now that they've reached the pinnacle of success, they've drifted apart—a fact demonstrated by TJ's "living like a Greek god" lifestyle.

Attempting to move on from his unrequited love for TJ, Freddie begins a relationship with the band's security guard. When the relationship takes a dark turn, his cymbals aren't the only things crashing.

After seeing Freddie's bruised face, TJ confesses his desperate longing to have Freddie back in his life—and his bed. Plus TJ knows he'll need his long time friend when cancer takes its toll on a loved one.

When these two lovers step into the Spotlight, they learn that money and fame can't save them from life's harsh realities and only together can they find the right rhythm.

Published by Green Moose Productions
Copyright 2019 by Jillian Jacobs
For sales information please contact: www.jillianjacobs.com

DEDICATION

To Queen. May your music always be my muse.

ACKNOWLEDGMENTS

To my beta team. Your input, as always, put the Spotlight right where it needed to be.

ONE

PRESENT DAY

SHIFTING ON THE COUCH DUE TO A NERVE-INDUCED COLD sweat trickling down his back, Freddie Davis tugged down the sleeve of his black suit jacket. He'd completed the modern-professional look with black designer jeans and a light pink tour T-shirt, which was emblazoned with the Apollo logo—a square-jawed Greek god with a lyre tattooed on his neck.

Freddie had recently refurbished the couch to a softer yellow fabric because all of TJ's black art-deco-over-priced furniture hadn't been built to withstand rowdy couch sex. This bi-level home in the Hill Section of Manhattan Beach had a glorious Pacific Ocean view. After moving in six months ago, he'd repainted the walls in various shades of yellow, and he'd added purple accent pillows, vases, and floral arrangements. A sunnier vibe—more of a home. He'd even worked with the landscapers to modify the pool area with a pond and waterfall, creating a soothing, trickling rhythm over the rocks during quiet evenings spent at home. Creating peace, something he'd fought very hard to attain.

He swallowed hard and blinked against the glare of the early morning sunlight blasting through the full wall of windows in his California home.

To everyone else, including the dainty blonde reporter currently sitting across from him, he was the drummer for Apollo, a pop rock band. A four-time-platinum-selling-album band. Billboard charts, music awards, and they'd even headlined the "big" game when the Marauders took the championship. Yet, around this time last year, he'd been beaten, bloody, and covered in disgusting fluids while on the floor of a 5-star hotel. All the money and fame hadn't kept him from being emotionally and physically ripped to pieces, but he'd picked himself back up, bit by bit and this interview would serve as a way to help others who had known the terror, shame, and fear of dealing with an abusive partner.

Rolling Rocker reporter, Ms. Roxy Burris re-crossed her legs and rocked her black stiletto back and forth. "I understand this topic can't be easy for you, Mr. Davis. I appreciate the exclusive." A pretty woman, as far as Freddie could tell, but his love of everything male meant women were washed with the same brush. Her legs were trim, and her plum-colored suit seemed a custom fit. She had tiny, cute features, and a nice puff of long blonde hair, descending around her shoulders.

Freddie wiped a damp hand against his pant leg and refocused on the interview. Burris had tilted her head a bit to the left, obviously wondering why he was gazing out the window instead of digging right in.

Clearing his throat, he said, "Speaking of the past isn't easy, no, but definitely necessary." He'd decided to do the interview on his own. No assistant. No PR team whispering the right answers in his ear. No agent. No lawyer. He'd stepped into this mess on his own, and after some intense therapy, he had to step out on his own. Unfiltered. Raw and real. The truth hurt, and by giving this interview, he'd lay everything out to be picked apart and reported on later, but the reality remained: Same–sex couples experienced domestic violence just like any other couple, and with men, it seemed a dirty secret or shameful, but...it wasn't. *It wasn't.*

"Then let's begin." Burris waved a hand, as if casting a spell to ease his mind during the long, sordid tale.

"Sure." He pulled a wood drumstick from beneath his leg, grabbed his other stick off the glass-topped coffee table, and tapped a beat against his thigh. He'd tried the carbon fiber sticks, but nothing was quite like the feel of hickory in his hand. He smirked, or perhaps, he just liked wood.

Ms. Burris sniffed and shuffled her mini-lap top against her thigh. "How about you begin when you met Kyle?"

He shivered as he recalled removing his bruised face from a hard, unforgiving carpet. Remembered showering off Kyle's punishment and looking in the mirror and seeing someone he didn't recognize. Someone broken. The first time his boyfriend had solved an argument with his fists, Freddie considered for a moment Kyle's statement that men resolved their issues through tough love. Hadn't his father always said to toughen up? To be a man. Those thoughts had clashed together and led Freddie to accept something unacceptable.

"Actually...I should go back further. The why of it all still eludes me, like why I let things get so bad, and...I-I don't know." Grimacing as his face heated, he scratched his temple. "But yeah... I'd like to start at the tipping point. Everything is important and yet at the same time, I don't know that I'll ever be able to fully explain why. I can write how I feel in lyrics. I can have TJ sing it, but this"—he flicked a hand between them—"this is hard and...I-I just want to help other men, you know? We *can* talk about intimate partner violence. It's okay. We're not less because we've been hit."

"I agree, and that's why we're here."

"Right." He sucked in a deep breath, wishing TJ was at his side. Wishing, he hadn't run off his best friend and lover this morning, saying he needed to do this on his own. He glanced at his iPhone on the table, maybe...

The security system's door alarm chimed, announcing someone entering the kitchen through the garage. Freddie's heartbeat kicked up like it always did when TJ arrived. A gorgeous man with sharp facial features and dark brown hair, styled to perfection with teasing, light brown eyes that always looked right through him. The happy-warm feeling in his chest was no different than the day they'd met eighteen years ago.

The love of his life poked his head around the kitchen wall and waved. "Hey."

Of course, TJ wouldn't stay away. He loved the fame part of their lifestyle. Loved talking about the band—and himself. His energy and enthusiasm could be exhausting, but Freddie wouldn't have him any other way.

Unwilling to voice—or show his relief, Freddie bit his bottom lip before tipping his drumstick in TJ's direction. "Why are you here?"

Not only was he here, he was alone—a rare thing for Apollo's lead singer who employed a long list of extraneous people. Sure, Freddie had an entourage, but nothing like TJ. He held interest in a few restaurants, a tequila brand, and a clothing line that mostly featured the Apollo logo but was branching out. He'd even done a guest-stint on a TV talent show a few years ago, but said that wasn't his thing. Which really equated to his love of sleeping in more than anything else.

TJ frowned and flicked a hand in the air. "I live here remember."

"Right." Freddie shook his head at how happy that truth made him while taking in the sexy man's artfully ripped jeans and slightly-faded-to-gray Apollo tour T-shirt, which was stretched taut across TJ's buff chest. The guy exuded sex. No one, certainly not Freddie, could have anything other than a visceral reaction to this man. TJ obviously noticed his thorough once-over and simply arched a dark, well-sculpted brow.

"Something on your mind, Freddie?"

"Something is always on my mind." He blinked away thoughts of what they'd done just this morning. The rawness of it all. The scents he hadn't wanted to wash off his skin. Feigning indifference, he waved a drumstick toward the bedroom. "Go away, please. I'm trying to do this interview." Keeping track of TJ out of his peripheral vision, Freddie faced the reporter, who now had a pen stuck to the bottom lip of her wide-open mouth.

Yeah, lady. He has that affect on everyone. Freddie refrained from rolling his eyes.

TJ sauntered into the room, feet bare, sexy toes on display before he stood in front of Freddie, blocking the reporter without ever acknowledging her existence. Always a bit of a selfish dick, his TJ.

"You okay?"

Freddie shrugged then said, "Okay is a very relative term."

"Jesus, Fred, I told you I'd do this with you." He crossed both arms over his chest, showing off his bulging biceps.

"I guess." Freddie tried redirecting his gaze from the package hidden behind TJ's well-worn jeans. If the reporter weren't here, he'd tug down that zipper and reveal what lay beneath. He licked his lips but then sighed. "Don't you have something else to do?"

"Nope." TJ sank down next to him, plopping his feet on the coffee table, which nudged aside a set of fall candles Freddie had artfully arranged just this morning.

Scowling at TJ, he simply shoved his lover's foot aside and fixed the set.

After snickering, TJ jerked his head toward the reporter. "So, where you at?"

The woman blinked then took a deep breath. "Oh my God! I'm so sorry." She exhaled in a rush. "This is so unprofessional, but I'm a huge fan." She bit down on the pen in her mouth, likely envisioning TJ's cock in its place.

"Most people are." TJ huffed out a laugh, then glanced back at Freddie. "But, let's focus on Fred, okay?"

Ha! Not too long ago, TJ would've smiled suggestively and flirted, but he'd changed. He really had. Freddie grinned and thanked God for that truth, because, well...it'd taken them far too long to get here.

"Right, of course." Ms. Burris flipped her hair over her shoulder. "We were...ah...let me see...Mr. Davis wanted to start at the beginning."

"Whoa, going all the way back, Fred?" TJ took his hand and squeezed.

Freddie ducked his chin because that simple touch did things to his heart. Always had. "I doubt I'll go back to grade school. She doesn't want to hear about our childhood."

"You two grew up together in..." She glanced at her notes. "Oak Brook, Illinois, right?"

TJ glanced at Freddie, and then cupped the side of his face. "That's ours and ours alone. Don't go that far back, Daz. Start at the hotel."

Freddie's heart warmed at TJ's nickname. In an attempt to fit in with the other boys at school, they'd started reading Marvel comics. At the time, Freddie was more interested in the Greek gods, but Dazzler—an obscure female mutant who could convert sound vibrations into light and energy beams—had caught his eye in the thin paper books he'd bought at the used bookstore. The character resonated as they were both blonde, blue-eyed beauties with musical aspirations. All his life, Freddie had lived up to the Dazzler title. He *could* convert words into light and energy. Every time his band took the stage, he glimpsed the "dazzle" in the fans' eyes.

He met TJ's brown-eyed gaze. "I planned to start at the hotel."

"Okay." TJ nodded, swallowing hard. "I'm so proud of you for doing this."

Overcome with love, Freddie lunged forward, gripped TJ's face, and kissed him with a loud smack. With their lips inches apart, he grinned. "I get to do that whenever I want now."

"You do." TJ grinned back. "You want me to stay?"

"Can you? *Without* interrupting?"

"No."

Fighting a smile again, Freddie pressed his hand against TJ's thrumming heart. "Yes, I want you to stay."

TJ ran a thumb along his cheek then flashed a cocky, I-know-what's-happening-in your-pants grin, before winking and turning to the reporter. "About a year ago, this guy was..."

"Hey!" Shaking off the lusty-haze, Freddie pressed a finger across TJ's million-dollar mouth. "Listen here, you glory hound, this is *my* story, and I'll tell it *my* way."

"You're wrong." He tipped Freddie's chin in his direction, his eyes blazing with so much love and understanding that Freddie almost whimpered. "It's *our* story, but I'll let you begin."

Freddie kept TJ's gaze for a moment longer, the rightness of his long-time love for this man distracting him from the focus of this very serious interview.

He turned to Ms. Burris, who had a soft smile on her face. For a second, he wondered what she would write about them, if she would redirect the interview's focus to their more sensational relationship rather than his true topic. Nothing for it now, he'd made his choice.

Freddie took a deep breath. "Well, TJ's staying." And didn't that just make him feel warm inside, because after waiting a very long time, TJ *was* staying. Gaze locked on the man he'd always loved, Freddie smiled and said, "Let's continue."

TWO

INTERVIEW

"ALL RIGHT, MS. BURRIS." FREDDIE GRIPPED BOTH DRUMSTICKS tight in his hand. "I'll start with what happened in Chicago. I'll start...with Kyle."

18 MONTHS AGO

Freddie held a hand against his bruised ribs as he slowly rose and sat on the side of the rumpled hotel bed. Wincing, he slowly got to his feet and shuffled to the bathroom. He held back a gag at the dried and crusty cum peeling off his side. He'd been punched, kicked, and then Kyle had knelt over him and jacked off, claiming he'd mark Freddie forever as his.

As a former member of the Army's Military Police Corps, maybe Kyle didn't know how to handle disagreements any other way? Maybe he considered Freddie his prisoner or something he had to fight to keep? Maybe they should try couple's therapy? Or maybe Freddie should just give up the idea of anything with this man, because he couldn't move without wincing.

The cause of Kyle's rage had been something so small. So insignificant.

A male fan had won backstage passes from a local radio station's contest, and upon meeting Freddie; he'd been suggestive, brushing up against him as often as possible. Freddie understood why people wanted him. His looks were above par. Not that he could help that he'd been born with good genes. Kyle even called him Angel. At six-two, with blond hair, blue eyes, and yes, Freddie would even say he had a finely sculpted face, almost too pretty—the kind of face featured on shaving cream advertisements, well...this fan's attraction made sense. Plus, Freddie *did* use quality skin products and perhaps splurged a little on the hair styling products, as well. A Dazzler had to Dazzle after all. RuPaul said, *"When you become the image of your own imagination, it's the most powerful thing you could ever do."* And Freddie lived on the gospel RuPaul. He'd grown up in awe of the fierce queen.

What would RuPaul say now, though? Freddie didn't look like an angel, more of a puffy-pink demon-spawn. The side of his face had a bright red imprint the size of Kyle's fist, which would fade into a rainbow of ghastly colors.

And what would Freddie say to TJ?

Freddie's stomach clenched at the thought of lying to TJ and his band mates—again. The shame of it all dropped him to his knees. He leaned over the toilet, sure all his stomach's contents were about to expel into the water below. The cold white tiles dug into his bare knees, and he sucked in a breath. "So gross. Toilets are gross no matter the number of stars a hotel has. So nasty." He blinked back tears. Even talking hurt. He sniffed and wiped a hand across his dripping nose.

The door key alarm beeped.

Oh God no! Was Kyle back?

A cold sweat cloaked his body, and his heart raced like mad. His mouth instantly dry as he tried to croak out a scream...something... anything. Where was his phone? He'd call someone. Someone would help, right? Did Siri recognize screams that really meant, I'm-dying-come-save-me? Yet, he remained frozen in place, clenching the sides of the toilet as heavy boots sounded on the carpet then stopped in the doorway. Maybe if he didn't move his predator wouldn't see him.

Kyle sat on the Jacuzzi tub and placed a hand on the back of Freddie's neck.

Shivering, Freddie tried to ease away, but Kyle just tightened his grip.

After a moment of tense silence, Freddie inched away from the toilet's rim, which was a dicey proposition, as his skin remained clammy, and he had to swallow the rising bile.

Kyle ran a hand down his back.

Freddie flinched. "Please," he whispered in a rough voice he'd never imagined coming from his mouth. "Don't touch me."

"I'm sorry, Freddie. It's just...you're just...you're beautiful, do you know that? It's bad enough you're up there in front of thousands of people drumming and sweating, and just...you weren't wearing a shirt, practically naked and then...and then you come backstage and that guy was all over you...you disrespected me and our relationship in front of all those people. You know we're together so why did you encourage that guy?"

"I didn't do anything wrong." Freddie sniffed and then folded his hands together in his lap. "And your apologies won't work. This is the second time you've hit me."

"And I explained I had to stake my claim." Kyle ran a hand through his dark brown hair before kneeling in front of Freddie.

"We've been together long enough that I shouldn't have to explain this anymore. I'm trying to make our relationship work, and I thought you were too. But no, you chose to make a fool of me instead, and I can't allow that."

Freddie had been on the receiving end of verbal abuse before. His father—a high and mighty religious zealot had been very un-Christian like in his verbiage relating to his son's sexuality. But this physical abuse, though similar and manipulative and biting, this abuse came with visible wounds. But just like after his father's tirades, Freddie had tried to rationalize the abusive behavior. Even forgiven Kyle the first time, but forgiveness didn't mean acceptance, and he'd already lived as a verbal punching bag for this father, he wouldn't do physical abuse for a boyfriend. Not happening. This relationship, and all the hopes that had come with it, were nothing but a faded dream.

He lifted his chin and met Kyle's gaze. He'd walked away from his father, and he would do the same with this man. The mental scars his father had left were far more painful than even Kyle's beefy fists. He could be strong, and maybe someday he'd find someone who didn't think him weak because he was gay or because he was pretty or whatever the reason was that he'd become such an easy target for hateful people.

Kyle's brown eyes were darker than TJ's—more chocolate than soft caramel. His black T-shirt with security in white block letters on the back still smelled of sweat from his night patrolling the arena and likely his jack-off session after he'd knocked Freddie to the floor and ejaculated on his crumpled body. If *that* was Kyle's way of marking his territory, then Freddie would pass. Getting off on another person's pain was demented.

"Listen." Kyle placed his big paws on Freddie's shoulders. "I'll try, I promise. Don't give up on me. We've been together too long to stop now. Things are going so great." He nodded his head as if expecting Freddie to just pick up the rhythm and agree.

Easing back as far as he could go, but not wanting to end up behind the toilet, Freddie swallowed hard and steeled his heart. "You hit me then you...you...came on me." He shivered and wished he weren't so naked, both physically and emotionally. And he needed a double dose of painkiller, like right now. "What you did is not okay, Kyle. It's actually very disturbing. You need to see someone about your anger issues. And until you do...w-we need to take a break." He risked a glimpse at Kyle, hoping his words wouldn't set the man off again. Chills ran down his spine at the thought. There was strong, and then there was stupid, and Freddie was anything but stupid. He knew to ease away from an angry bear, not prod and poke it with a stick.

"If that's what you need, then fine, I will see someone." Kyle reached over and squeezed Freddie's thigh. "I love you so much, and I'll do anything to prove it. Plus, you know I'm sorry. I was just playing around. Things got a little heated. It happens." He tugged Freddie onto his lap and pressed him against his bulging chest muscles. "I won't let you go."

The tight hold shot pain like a pinball across Freddie's face, first along this cheek, then his temple, before landing in some fantastic pain receptor in his brain. "I-I need some space."

Kyle tensed and he practically growled his words. "I just told you I would fix this, where do you think you're going now?"

"I'm not doubting you. I-I'm *afraid* of you." Freddie stared across the bathroom at the framed art above the toilet. A lighthouse, resting upon a pile of rocks. That's what he needed, the hope that something would keep him away from further storms. Storms that held lightning and thunder. Storms that woke him at night when they struck with loud booms and bright flashes of light. Storms that came from the man beside him and scared him so badly he wanted to hide away forever.

"You're afraid of me?" Kyle's deep voice took on an almost childlike tone.

"Yes." Freddie blinked away tears. Furious with himself for remaining in this beast's arms. Why wasn't he running for the door? Why was he still frozen in place? "I'd like to take a shower now. Could you just...just go, please?"

Kyle grasped Freddie's hands in his own. "I lose my mind around you. Let me try to get better, please?"

Freddie looked into Kyle's eyes. Kyle was five years younger than his twenty-eight. Young, rash, and fresh out of the military, perhaps he'd been around violence too long and didn't know how to handle conflict any other way.

Freddie could be compassionate. Maybe he could help Kyle change for the better. And he *had* cared for the man. "I'll talk to Pepper about finding someone for you to talk to, b-but...but that's all."

Kyle frowned. "I can't run off and just *talk* to people. My job is the band's safety."

After reflecting on that ridiculous statement in light of this very unsafe situation, Freddie chose his next words carefully. "That includes *my* safety, right?"

Kyle nodded. "Of course."

"Then, I won't budge on this. You either talk to someone or we're through. I won't be hit again, Kyle. I won't." *Never again.* Freddie made that mental promise to himself, because other than Kyle's temper, they meshed really well. And he craved that because the one person he'd loved his whole life was moving further and further away every day. TJ had changed so much. Fame had gone to his head, and they were no longer close. Freddie had cried over it, tried to change things, but TJ loved living like a rock star, which meant any hopes of their happily ever after had crashed and died.

So, when Kyle had come along and treated him like a queen, he'd finally decided to move on. But now? Now, he'd have to pack up his heart and move on again.

Freddie's heart still ached over the continued disconnect between him and TJ, and he wanted nothing more than to trust his old friend again. Yet over and over since they began this journey together, TJ had broken his heart. More like, ripped it from his chest and kicked it across the stage. Perhaps Kyle had always sensed that Freddie had never truly been all-in.

Freddie sighed and pressed against Kyle's grip. "I'm taking a shower then some aspirin and going to bed." Not that he'd ever be warm again based on the frigidness of his body. How would he ever feel safe? What would Kyle say if he asked for the room key back? And even worse, what if Kyle wanted to stay and sleep with him? He shivered. He'd get a different room and just not tell anyone. Yeah, right, he was monitored 24-7, that'd never fly. "Listen, Kyle, we have five more stops on this tour, so we'll put a Band-Aid on this for now, but if you hit me again or do anything violent, I'll have you arrested for assault. Now, I'd like some privacy. Please do me the courtesy of staying in another room tonight." He held his breath, hoping his stern words didn't provoke another beating.

Standing, Kyle braced his arms across his burly chest and nodded. "If that's what you think you need, Freddie. Even though you're being your usual drama queen self about everything." He shook his head, jaw clenched. "I'll stay with Bruce tonight."

Bruce was Apollo's head of security. TJ had hired him because Bruce literally looked like Bruce Willis. Who better to yippee-ki-yay their fans?

Kyle left the bathroom, but Freddie waited until he heard the door shut before grabbing a heated towel off the rack, wrapping it around his body, and turning on the shower.

He avoided looking in the mirror again. Mirrors held far too many truths, and he refused to catch another glimpse of the broken and absolutely terrified man staring back at him.

He bit his bottom lip, hard, and tried to focus on that pain. Tears fell and he slid onto the floor and cried until not one drop of anything remained.

THREE

"I HAVE TO INTERJECT." TJ GRIPPED FREDDIE'S HAND.

"Sure." Ms. Burris diverted her attention to him, smile wide.

"I didn't know about any of this. I was living the dream, and my best friend, he was...he was being hurt...and I just didn't know..."

TJ HELD UP HIS PHONE AND HIT LIVE ON HIS FACEBOOK PAGE'S feed. "Hey, Chicago! My favorite city in the world! Sorry, but it *is* my hometown. We're all set up for rehearsal this morning. I was outside earlier, and it was hot as hell out there. I do *not* miss the Midwest's humidity." He spun in a circle, letting his phone take in the entire amphitheater including a quick flash of his assistant Jared, who was on his phone doing something, as always. "Anyway, who cares about the weather? Tonight's gonna be lit." He stuck out his tongue and riffed a little of "Angry Hearts" the band's latest hit.

"Speaking of angry? Where's Freddie? Ah, he's over by his precious drums, fucking around." TJ headed that way, flipping the screen.

His best friend had always fit seamlessly into his life. His family even liked Freddie better than him most of the time. When TJ was eight, his father had walked away from his wife and three kids. Two years later, after moving and changing schools, TJ had met Freddie, which was the only bright spot of the time.

As the only man in the house, he'd appointed himself the caretaker role, and even now, he couldn't stop. With all the fame and money and bullshit, he still felt the pressure to keep his family warm and fed. He remembered that dull ache in his empty belly, and his cold feet when his mom couldn't pay the gas bill. Money made life easier. Fame made life fun. But...this cancer nightmare with his sister, Emily...

Cancer didn't care about money. Cancer just laughed and burned through every penny, mocking him as he tossed more dollar bills onto the flames. His money changed nothing just left him cold and powerless, and Emily, she just stayed sick.

Shaking off that thought, he zoomed in on the hot blond behind the drums. "And here's Freddie Davis everyone. Just look at that sexy ass." TJ marched around and licked his lips. Freddie always reminded TJ of those sculpted marble statues that represented everything beautiful about the male form. Plus, those statues were set high on pedestals, surrounded by security rope, and unattainable. That was Freddie—untouchable beauty. Not that they hadn't touched. In high school, they'd given in to their hormonal curiosities, but then...well, what the hell had he thought? TJ was roadside gravel, while Freddie was shiny marble, gleaming under the spotlight. All blond hair, striking blue eyes, and a lean, yet fit body. And those well-defined arms that could probably jack a guy's dick for days without tiring. *Fucking hell.* Now his cock was dripping—something that occurred every time sex with Freddie came to mind.

"Fred, hey, whatcha doin'?" TJ waited for Freddie to turn around, but the stubborn, self-declared hater of social media stayed bent over, fiddling with the small mic over the snare drum. Freddie hated when TJ did live videos, selfies, or anything on social media. But his drummer was oh, so photogenic and the fans loved that shit.

While hot-as-hell in his own ways, TJ knew he was a little rougher around the edges, with dirty dark-blond hair, light brown eyes, and a few inches taller than Freddie's six-two, plus he was a bit beefier—everywhere. He smirked.

In the past, he'd used that bulk to protect his best friend but they'd drifted apart lately, not that TJ blamed him. He'd created the distance with his wild ways, but didn't know how to fix it, and that...hurt. So he made it worse by drowning his feelings in sex and other unmentionables. "Hey, Daz, smile at us with those bright, white teeth and say hi."

Freddie mumbled something unintelligible, so TJ stomped around the drums and nudged his friend's shoulder. "He's always so shy. You ready for tonight?"

Freddie shoved out a hand then hissed out a breath. "Mmmh-mm." He placed a hand against his side. "Get that phone out of my face."

Frowning, TJ flipped the phone's camera around. "See what I have to deal with." He released an exaggerated sigh. "He's grumpy as fuck *all* the time." Shaking his head, he glanced back at Freddie. "And here I thought getting laid on a frequent basis would fix that." He laughed though he'd never really thought the whole Kyle—aka Juggernaut—relationship was humorous or interesting or the least bit right for Freddie, but no one had asked him. *Fuckers.* He cupped a hand by his mouth and whispered a secret to his fans like he was imparting the biggest news ever. "Freddie has a new man. I call him Juggernaut. He's this big beefy security guard." He grunted. "Bet I know what they do with the zip ties." Waggling his brows, he watched all the Likes and messages pop up on his screen. Lots of hearts and declarations of love. Even one offer of a threesome with him and Freddie. That'd be intense, but Freddie was in "lurve" with Kyle. He frowned, not liking that thought at all. "I better get to work. I'll check in tonight before the show. Love you!"

He clicked off and shoved his phone in the back pocket of his jeans.

Time to annoy Freddie.

Tugging up his low-slung jeans, he poked Freddie's shoulder. "Hey, want to grab a coffee or some chocolate? You sound like you need something sweet, and we both know how much chocolate makes you smile." He'd chuckled but instantly sobered when he glimpsed the dark purple bruise on the side of Freddie's face. "What is *that*?" Anger spiking, he gripped Freddie by the chin.

Freddie yanked away. "Stop. It's nothing."

TJ narrowed his eyes, "Like hell it's nothing."

Freddie's gaze dropped to the bolt on his kick drum.

What was *that* face? Embarrassment? Why were his cheeks turning red? Freddie had always shared everything with TJ. No matter what. They'd built this band from scratch into the mega-music phenomenon it was today, and now his friend was unwilling to share the truth? "Daz, what happened to you?"

Freddie scoffed. "As if you care."

"Don't throw that shit in my face."

"It's not a big deal."

TJ locked both hands on his hips and glared at Freddie. "Wait a minute...didn't you have a similar bruise a month ago?" He glanced around looking for Kyle because that asshole was going down. "Is he hitting you or something? What the fuck, Fred?"

Blue eyes wide, Freddie stepped away from his drums and gripped TJ's arm. "Stay out of it. I'm handling things."

"Things?" TJ's stomach sank, because, *What the hell?* He'd had his suspicions the first time Freddie had shown up with a bruise because that smug fucker, Kyle kept Freddie all to himself. All the signs were there. TJ should know, he'd seen his Mom get corralled by a couple abusive boyfriends during his childhood. No way was he letting the whole, because-I'm-the-man-I can-hit-you shit happen to Freddie. "Getting hit is *not* a *thing*. Kyle is fired. Done. I'm not having it." He spun on his heel and glanced through all the stupid people milling around backstage for whatever reason. Rising up on his toes, he struggled for a glimpse of their manager, Pepper or even Bruce. Why were they on his ass when he didn't need them but magically absent when he did? "Jared! Where is Pepper, or even better, get Bruce!" His assistant had startled at this tone but then scampered off.

"Oh, this is classic." Freddie rolled his eyes.

"What is?"

"Nothing."

"You can't say something is *classic* and then not explain. Quit being a dick."

"I can and I did."

TJ blinked, because, *what?* "You have no idea what you're doing or saying, obviously." He waved a hand at Freddie's bruised face. "And if that's all the explanation you can see fit to give then I have no choice but to fire that thug."

Freddie huffed out a laugh. "It's *classic* because you've hurt me far worse...many, many times."

"What? When?" But he knew, of course he knew. Their troubles had nothing to do with that bruise on Freddie's face though...or did it? He likely had some blame somewhere, but he'd be damned if he'd let Freddie throw anything back in his face when his life-long friend stood there practically glowing purple. "Don't try to change the subject or put this on me somehow. You want to talk about us then we can talk about us, but not now. Right now, we're dealing with your face and Kyle. End of story."

Freddie stared at him for a moment but then sighed and ran his fingers through that thick blond hair that was longer on top and tended to curl if he didn't tame it with product. A whiff of the lavender-scented shampoo Freddie used drifted through the air. His drummer had a thing for everything purple. Always had.

"TJ, *our* relationship is *strictly* professional, so I'm sorry, but at this point, you have no say in my personal life. I never even said Kyle did this...so, let's stay on track." He turned away. "We have to rehearse this morning, so let's focus on that."

TJ gripped Freddie's shoulder and turned him around. What he wanted was to wrap this man in his arms, but for some reason, he held back. Always held back. *Gravel and marble, they'd always be.* "A *strictly* professional relationship after everything we've done together, that's what you're going with?"

"What else would I go with?"

Me.

Freddie was supposed to say he'd go anywhere and do anything with *me*. And *his* Freddie would've said that at one time. Yet during their rise to fame, they'd become strangers. TJ had to fix things, because obviously Freddie was making a mess of his life if his face was any indication. "Let me be clear about this, we do not have a *professional* relationship, we have an *everything* relationship. We're X-Men and Greek gods. We're Apollo. We're peas and carrots and grape jelly and peanut butter. You know this. Friends forever and all that." He braced a hand around the back of Freddie's neck, ignoring the smoothness of his skin and how that simple touch melted his heart in a way nothing else ever had. "Now, tell me what happened to your face, and why you're holding your side like that, and I'll fix it like I always have and always will."

Shaking his head, Freddie jutted out his chin and met his gaze with those steely blue eyes blazing. "Did we have an *everything* relationship last month when the band won the American Music Award, and you stormed onto the stage, high as a kite, and grabbed the statue out of that poor actor's hand before storming off? You didn't wait for us to take the stage with you, and you certainly didn't party with us that night. So, no, we don't have *anything*."

That hit TJ in the gut, mostly because it was true. "I told you I was sorry, and that whole bad boy act...well, it sells records, doesn't it?"

Shoving away, Freddie continued to glare. "Do we have an *everything* relationship when you're talking to Rock Boots Records about a single album?"

"I told you I said no to them. What do you want from me?" TJ threw up both hands.

Freddie flinched and slipped to the side, raising his forearms to block his face.

A protective stance. A please-don't-hit-me stance.

"My God, Freddie. He *did* hit you." TJ stuck out a hand but quickly pulled it back when fear flared in Freddie's eyes. He hadn't wanted to actually believe his friend was being abused, but people didn't shy away and scrunch up like that if they weren't afraid. "Freddie, we can fix this. Kyle will go and you'll be safe again. It's going to be all right."

"Please, just stop." Freddie straightened and rolled his shoulders. "Put your face back in your phone, TJ. Go live in your universe. I don't need your help."

Ouch! So this was the state of things, was it? Fine. More than fine. Fuck fine. "Sure. Whatever you say, Fred. You do your thing. You just keep walking around with your face all bruised up and see if I give two shits." TJ gritted his teeth and stormed off.

Ignoring the looks of the sound crew, the lighting crew, and every other jerk that'd stopped what they were doing to watch the Freddie and TJ show, he stalked to his dressing room. What he wanted was a punching bag. Maybe he'd search out Kyle now.

Regardless of what Freddie thought he wanted, TJ *would* be talking to Kyle. And why wasn't Jared back yet?

Grumbling, he stopped short at the overabundance of people in his dressing room, yelled at everyone to get out, and then plopped onto the wide black leather recliner some minion had set up next to a well-used brown loveseat.

All right, so he *had* been a dick for a long time, but hell, this rock-star life was everything his dirt-poor ass had ever wanted. Plus, he had two younger sisters and his mom to support. Not to mention Emily's cancer. His sister had been hanging on by a thread for a lot longer than anyone predicted.

"Fuck." He ran a hand through this hair before banging his fist against the chair's arm. "What am I gonna do about you, Fred? Telling me I can't fix this. Well, I'll fix it all right. Kyle will never work in this industry again once I'm through with his abusive ass."

He'd been missing Freddie more and more lately. Even though they were together all the time, they weren't in synch. And that man with the hideous bruise on his face was the only "real" person in his life. They both had so much...just noise around them all the time, just people, and more people, and places to be seen and business to handle. He longed for the quiet moments with just him and Freddie, reading comic books, coming up with song lyrics, and playing video games together. He didn't know how to bridge that gap, or even if he should.

Freddie was light and beauty, and he was dark and dirty. And yet...he wasn't that kid with an empty belly and dollar store shoes anymore. He was the lead singer of Apollo, and he'd fought, and screamed, and ripped himself raw for what he wanted. And what he wanted was for Freddie Davis to love him again.

FOUR

"So, I'm pissed, right?" TJ edged forward on the couch, bouncing his knee. "I can't even see through all the red in my vision, but you know, life sometimes, it keeps throwing curveballs."

Freddie sat up and cupped TJ's chin, turning his face. "You don't need to do this."

"It's part of our story, and it helped you realize I needed you, right?"

"I guess it did that and a lot of other things..."

TJ hauled his butt out of the recliner and went to chew a hefty piece of Kyle's muscled ass—yes, he'd noticed and no, he wouldn't touch the Juggernaut Jerk for anything. His frustration only mounted as on his way to find Kyle, he was stopped by the light guys, the sound gal, and Pepper tried waving him over, but if he spoke to her, he'd likely go off, and he needed to handle the serious security breach evident all over Freddie's face by himself. He could go all rock star diva and have other people handle this mess, but this was personal and he wasn't afraid to fight. Hell, he'd been fighting for Freddie their whole lives whether or not the drummer still believed that truth though was another question all together.

And because Ares, the god of war was apparently against him, he growled out a sigh when his phone rang with his mom's ring tone. Only his family and band mates had the number to his personal line. Holding the phone to his ear, he answered, "What's up, Ma?"

"TJ, honey, hello. I was wondering if you're staying in Chicago for a bit after tonight's concert?"

"Ma, I told you, remember? We're wrapping up the tour in the Midwest on purpose so I could come home for a while."

"Oh." She sniffed. "That's right. I'm sorry."

"Do you have a cold? You sound congested?" He tightened his grip on the phone.

"No. It's Emily. She had a bad doctor visit."

"Bad in what way, Mom?" He shot through the back stage area, looking for Kyle, because that bastard's face would serve well as an outlet for this unease brewing in his gut. Metastatic cancer didn't end, just hung out, waiting to take Emily away, as if the Reaper stood over her all the time and lowered his blade inch by inch.

"When are you done with your tour?"

"We have five more stops in Indiana and Ohio after tonight. Why? What's going on with Emily?"

"Well...hmm...are they back to back nights or weekends? I'm sorry. I just don't remember."

"It's over the next two weeks. Two cities in Indiana, then three in Ohio then back home after that." TJ skidded to a stop in the middle of all the backstage chaos as a wave of fear rushed down his spine. A mass of people buzzed around him, but he only heard his mom's soft breathing along with her favorite country radio station playing in the background. "Why aren't you answering me about Em?"

His mom cleared her throat and sniffed again.

"God damn it! How bad?" Worry for his sister slid into his gut and he crouched down, trying to hold himself together.

"TJ, we didn't want to worry you."

"Fuck that. I'm out here busting my ass for you *and* for her, so don't say that to me."

"We weren't sure until today."

"That's still not fair. I deserved to know."

"You were busy."

"Never." He closed his eyes and blew out a long breath. "I'm *never* too busy for you. And I'm sick of this general consensus that I don't give a shit about anyone and should be left out of everything."

"TJ, I *did* leave you a message a week ago and you didn't call me back."

Brow drawn together, he sighed, because he couldn't remember any call from his mom. If Jared had been forgetting his messages again, he'd choke that fool. "If you did, I'm sorry. I'm messing everything up. I know that, but I'll be there. Let me see what we can do but I'll be there."

"It'll hold."

Anger roared through his system. He wished he could write lyrics like Freddie at times like these, just to release all the pain and anxiety banging around in his head. "*Cancer* doesn't hold for anyone or anything. It's an asshole, and I said I'd be there."

"Don't yell at me, young man. You may be able to talk to other people like that but I won't have it."

"Ma...."

"Yeah, don't *Ma* me."

"I'm sorry."

She grunted. "You'd better be."

"Ma..."

"Yeah."

"Why's it gotta be so hard?"

"Cause we're alive, baby. And there's nothing wrong with feeling. It's when you don't feel that something's wrong."

He took a deep breath and rushed out his confession. "Freddie doesn't like me anymore and his boyfriend is hitting him."

"Well...that's...I don't know what to say other than, what do you plan to do about it? Because if you don't fix things, believe me, I will. That boy and his family, well...his Mom anyway, they helped you and the band when I couldn't, so you fix this. Right now."

"I will." TJ bit his lip. Fuck if he'd start crying now. He wouldn't give up hope that life could change for the better, but damn, if life wasn't always pushing back. Yet this woman on the line—this strong, capable female—had always told him to reach for the stars, and he had, because she'd never let him believe anything else. His Ma was a tiny, bleached-blonde, with pretty brown eyes, and a fighter's heart. He loved her more than anything.

"Bring Freddie and come see your sister. I'm afraid time is a luxury we no longer have, kiddo."

"Jesus, Ma. What am I supposed to say to that?"

"Say, you'll be here. I need you here. Your sisters need you."

"I promise." He wiped a hand across his suddenly wet cheeks before breathing deeply. "Let me take care of what I need to here so I can be there without constant interruptions. I'll work it out."

"That's my boy."

"Love you," he croaked out, swallowing hard.

"Love you more."

Hanging up, TJ gazed at a small crack in the concrete floor, gathering his emotions and trying to stem the stupid tears leaking from his eyes. *Great.* He needed Freddie to ease this angry fire burning through his chest. They could go home together. Emily was as much Freddie's sister as his own. But TJ's grand plan had two major flaws: Freddie was in denial about his purple face *and* he hated TJ right now.

"Hey, TJ." Drake, the band's lead guitarist pressed a hand on his shoulder. "What are you doing?"

TJ glanced up at Drake. His band mate wore dark blue skinny jeans and a Mighty Mighty Bosstones T-shirt with his shoulder-length naturally curly blond hair tied up in a bun.

Drake knelt beside him. "We've been looking for you. The sound and light crews are ready." He tugged on TJ's arm, lifted him up, and led him back toward the stage.

"Stop a sec." TJ shrugged him off. "I have to talk to someone."

Arching a brow, Drake shook his head. "You looking for Kyle?"

"Maybe."

Drake frowned and then shoved him forward again. "I already saw Freddie's face. He said it wouldn't happen again, and that Kyle was going into therapy or something."

"The only thing that Juggernaut is *going into* is my fist."

"TJ, man, first of all, Kyle would destroy you. I mean you're street-tough but he's been trained and shit. Not to mention, you had your chance with Freddie, for *years*, and so no, you don't get a say now."

"The fuck I don't." TJ stopped and glared at Drake, hands on hips, because how could his guitarist just go on about his business when Freddie's business was a complete disaster?

"Kim and I talked to Bruce about Kyle."

Great. TJ groaned and ran a hand down his face. Although, he couldn't fault Kim and Drake's involvement, as other than his immediate family, they were the most important people in his and Freddie's life. "I'll be talking to Bruce as well about this being the second time Kyle's hit Freddie."

Drake glanced toward the stage then sighed. "Freddie needs to do this on his own."

"That's not how *we* work." TJ whipped a finger back and forth between them.

"Maybe in the beginning, but you've kinda...well, ya kinda burned that bridge."

TJ braced a hand on Drake's shoulder. "Oh, God, I can't do this. Freddie's all busted up, and Emily...is well, she's at the...the, you know...." He flicked a hand in the air, unable to say the word.

Drake drew him into a hug. "Ah, man. I'm so sorry. What do we need to do?"

And wasn't that how it'd always been. They were a team. The "we" being the most important thing. How had he let that slide for so long? "Thanks, I needed that." TJ eased out of Drake's hold. "*We* need to rock this concert tonight. We need to take better care of Freddie. We need to double-team Kyle's ass—and not in the fun way." He smirked then shook his head. "And then we need to call my sister's doctors, because, if we have to, we're cancelling the rest of the tour. I won't continue if she's...if...well...you know..."

"Then that's what we'll do."

The sympathy in Drake's tone cut him deep. He sucked in a breath and wished his band mate would hold him tight again. Hold him together because when he lost Emily, he'd simply break. "Yeah? You with me on this? Even if it means fighting with all the powers that be who'll just want us to finish the rest of the tour?"

"You just said, *we*, and our fans will understand even if all the rest of the money grubbers don't, you get me?" Drake punched his shoulder. "Breathe man. We'll get through this."

"I still want to punch Kyle's face."

Drake lips lifted and he shook his head. "Nah, you need to be pretty for all the pictures."

"Fuck the pictures."

"Says Mr. Instagram-my-ass-blossom."

"Oh my God, when will you guys stop giving me grief about that? It was for an *art* exhibit. "

"Dude, casting your ass pucker into a mold and putting it on display was for *your* narcissism. Not to mention so nasty." Drake shivered. "I didn't need to see that. I had to use eye wash for an hour."

"Many people enjoyed the beauty of my ass blossom." Grinning, he bumped said ass against Drake's hip.

"Many, many people have enjoyed your *real* ass blossom. Don't know why you had to share it as art."

TJ shrugged. "Too true."

Kim walked up beside them, her sleek black hair framing her oval face. "Why are you talking about TJ's ass blossom again?"

TJ heaved a heavy sigh. "The better question is, why are you giving me hell instead of getting ready for tonight?"

Kim smiled, the action lighting up her dark brown eyes before she kissed Drake on the cheek.

Drake, a husky guy about five-ten, with hazel eyes, seemed a mismatch to tiny Kim, but they'd been together for two years, even through all the craziness of fame. They were both homebodies who lived to play their guitars, so they meshed. They never discussed their relationship in interviews, protecting it as something sacred.

Yet if the relationship were between he and Freddie, TJ knew the constant public scrutiny would be non-stop. He'd be forced to change his share-everything-on-social-media lifestyle.

TJ wrapped his arms around both Drake and Kim, shuffling them forward. "All right, let's get to work. We'll rock Chicago then go see Emily."

Tonight's concert tickets had sold out in less than two hours so TJ had to set aside his personal issues and be a professional. With all the turmoil in his head and heart, he'd rip and roar through tonight's playlist. Singing always freed his soul and tonight, he needed that freedom and sweet release more than anything.

———

Eighteen years ago

Fourth Grade recess

Sitting in a semi-shady spot on the playground, Freddie *cringed as a large shadow fell across his wide-ruled notebook.*

Greg Jones yanked his notebook out of his hand. "Is the little fairy writing poetry again?"

"They're songs," Freddie mumbled, though his words were useless as he'd had this conversation with Greg-the-gross before.

"We need you to be Iceman." Greg yanked on Freddie's arm. "I'm Wolverine, and Matt is Cyclops."

"I don't want to play."

Greg yanked him up anyway. "If you don't get up, I'll throw this book away." He held the notebook over his head.

"How about you play, Odysseus? You know, like the Greek god in the Odyssey. *The book we're reading in class. That's way cooler than X-Men."*

Greg shoved his shoulder. "I bet you haven't even seen the movie."

Freddie dropped his gaze. He hadn't because his Mom didn't feel the content was age-appropriate. Plus he hadn't been interested in a super-hero movie. He was more into Greek gods and music than comic books. "Can I have my notebook back?"

"No. I'm Wolverine. I have to slice it." Greg ripped a page from the book.

Freddie's stomach churned. "Please don't do that." The notebook contained his stories of Apollo's adventures.

"What's going on over here?" The new kid, sporting a white T-shirt, high-water jeans, and non-brand tennis shoes came to stand at Greg's side.

Freddie had seen the dark blond kid with darker eyebrows during recess as he was in the other third grade class. He was just as big as Greg the Gross, and usually shot hoops with kids in his class.

The new kid ripped Freddie's notebook out of Greg's hand. "Quit being a dickhead."

Freddie gasped at the kid's bad word. He glanced around to see if a teacher overheard.

Greg shrugged. "Want to play X-Men? You can be Magneto?"

"Nah." The kid shrugged as he sank down next to Freddie. "I'm good."

Greg and his buddy scampered off.

The kid looked over the pages in Freddie's notebook. "You like the Greek gods?"

"Yes," Freddie answered in a small voice.

"Me too." The boy flipped through his pages some more. "We don't have cable so mom lets us get books, and sometimes movies, at the library."

Freddie couldn't imagine life without a hundred different channels or his PlayStation 2—a recent gift for getting good grades. "Why don't you have cable?"

"No money."

"Oh." Freddie glanced at the kid's face and a weird feeling stirred in his tummy. Maybe he was hungry. "What's your name?"

"TJ."

"Oh, I'm Freddie. Can I have my notebook back, please?"

"What's this?" He pointed to the pencil drawing of a bright purple lyre.

"It's a lyre, like a small harp."

"Right, like the one Apollo has, the god of music."

Freddie's heart beat faster, and he grinned. "Yes, exactly. D-do you like music?"

TJ grinned back before handing over the notebook. "Of course, I do."

Oh boy! Right then and there, Freddie hoped as he'd never hoped before that he'd finally made a true friend.

FIVE

"I wish you'd told me about Emily before the concert."
Freddie fiddled with the pumpkin spice scented candle in his fall
arrangement.

"You weren't exactly happy with me right then."

"You were so on that night, but at the time, I thought maybe you
were pumped because we were back in Chicago."

"No, that wasn't the reason at all."

Soaked in sweat after a grueling three-hour concert,
TJ chugged down a bottle of water. He'd belted out the lyrics,
releasing everything ripping through his heart. He'd always done
that, sang at the top of his lungs. Music was his saving grace. As a
little kid, his father had smacked him around whenever he sang a
"girly" song, so he'd switched to grittier rock, which suited his voice
better anyway.

He wiped the sweat from his face and turned to find Freddie so
he could apologize for whatever would get them started on the right

track again. After singing from his very soul, he was always a little emotional so why not start the healing process while caught in that vibe. Ignoring all the people milling around back stage, he scanned the area until he spotted shiny blond hair and hollered, "Hey, Freddie. Wait up."

Freddie's shoulders hunched, but he turned around, his left brow arching high. "What is it, TJ?"

His friend's cheek was a darker purple mixed with red now, which just pissed TJ off again. "Let's head back to my dressing room for a few. Rehydrate and maybe bang out a few games of *God of War*."

Freddie twirled his drumsticks before stuffing them in his back pocket. Sweat dripped down his bare torso leading to his happy trail. Fucking hell, he was perfect. In every way. Sculpted so beautifully.

TJ chewed on his bottom lip, unsure where to start...though, he'd like to start by licking the sweat from Freddie's body. In an attempt to calm his lustful thoughts, he pressed the cool water bottle against his heated cheeks.

Freddie wiped his chest with the white T-shirt in his hand. "I need to get showered and rest."

His words were muffled as he tugged the T-shirt over his head.

"It's about Emily."

"Oh no, what happened?" Free from his shirt, Freddie immediately stepped forward.

TJ opened his mouth to answer but then his entire body shot to red-alert as Kyle strolled up to Freddie, holding a water bottle. "Here you go. Get rehydrated."

TJ shoved Kyle's shoulder. "Back the hell up, man. First off, we were having a private discussion. Second, you're done as soon as I speak to Bruce. Done." He bumped his chest against Kyle's much bulkier mass. "You hurt Freddie so you're fired. And I'll make sure everyone knows exactly what you are. Good luck finding work again in this field."

Kyle shoved him back. "Get out of my face."

TJ swung, but he'd forgotten about the open water bottle in his hand, so his fist *and* the water went flying.

Kyle blocked his right cross with a raised forearm then grabbed the water bottle, crumpled it, and tossed it to the ground.

Adrenaline and absolute fury firing his blood, TJ surged forward again. "I will end you."

"Stop." Freddie stepped in front of TJ and placed both hands on his shoulders, pressing him back. "That's enough."

TJ kept his gaze on Kyle. "No, it isn't."

Without dropping his gaze, Kyle flicked water from his arm.

"TJ, calm down, okay? No more violence. Please."

TJ glanced into Freddie's eyes, caught the silent plea and sighed. He stepped back but kept his feet braced apart, ready to spring into action.

Freddie raked his fingers through his sweaty hair before turning to Kyle. "Thank you for the water, Kyle, but TJ and I *were* having a private discussion, so please excuse us." He turned his back on Kyle and took a long draw from the water bottle.

"Freddie, we need to talk." Kyle cleared his throat. "When you're done here. In *our* room."

TJ practically ripped his neck in half, whipping around to gawk at the guy. "Are you *insane?* I *just* said, you're fired. Go the hell away. Now! Two strikes, asshole, and in my book, that means you're out."

"TJ, enough."

Freddie's tone came across very stern and highly irritated. Not a version TJ was used to.

"I told you that Kyle and I are not your concern."

Grumbling a few choice curses, TJ blew out a long breath then caught a glimpse of Drake and Kim standing off to the side. Kim was yelling at a couple people who had their phone's cameras pointed toward their fight. Drake stood at her side, hands on hips while his tiger jabbed a finger at the offending photogs. Great, this fight would go viral soon.

TJ turned back to Freddie and tried to keep his tone level to avoid further interest in their little drama. "You *are* my concern, but sure, whatever, you say, *Daz*. You just keep on shining with that purple face of yours." He glared at Kyle before hooking a thumb over his shoulder. "You can go now, *Kyle*. No one needs you here, and I will be discussing your behavior with Bruce. Pack your bags, jackass."

"TJ." Freddie shook his arm. "Stop it. I'm handling this."

Kyle edged closer. "Freddie, don't listen to him. He doesn't care about anyone but himself. We've talked about this."

Oh, they'd talked about this? And just what the heck was *this*? TJ scoffed before rounding on this unbelievably forward jerk. "Listen, you may be able to take me, but know this, I'll do plenty of damage before you do. Back off!" He stepped around Freddie into Kyle's space again.

Drake appeared at TJ's side and placed a hand on his shoulder. "Hey, come on. Let's all step back a moment."

TJ flicked a hand in the air. "No, let's *not* step back. He needs my foot up his ass and then to pack his shit and get the fuck out of my face."

Drake turned to Kyle. "Listen, could you just go? Give everyone some space, please?"

TJ hoped he'd stay. Hoped Kyle would say just one more thing to Freddie because though TJ would likely lose the fight, he was angry enough not to care. He hadn't fought in a long time, but he would. He'd do anything to protect Freddie. Always had.

Kyle chose that moment to have some sense and stomped off to

God knew where. They watched him leave for a moment and then Drake squeezed TJ's arm.

"You got a death wish, bro. Come on. Let's go get something to drink." Drake eased between him and Freddie as they all shuffled to the green room.

Freddie sighed as he stepped across the threshold.

TJ headed for a metal tub filled with ice and water bottles, pulling one out of the very bottom.

"TJ, listen to me. I appreciate you trying to protect me, but Kyle promised he'd speak to someone about his anger issues. I don't think he knows how to handle his feelings any way other than violence."

TJ twisted off the water bottle's cap a little harder than necessary. "So he just gets to hit you and that's that. He gets, what? A free pass to do it again?"

"No, I just said, he's getting help. Now drop it." Freddie shook his head and then took a long drink from the water bottle Kyle had brought him.

TJ wanted to rip it from his hand and give him a new one, but he was too entranced by the plump lips wrapped around the water bottle. He'd kissed those sweet lips before. They were nice lips. Perfect lips. An overwhelming urge to take them again shot straight from his brain to his dick. He wanted to feel that cold, wet tongue brush against his own. He squirmed, pressing a flat palm against his thickening dick.

But, Drake was here, and TJ had a million texts and calls coming across on his work phone. He hadn't liked the lighting for the second song. Needed to make plans to see Emily. Needed to find Bruce to fire Kyle and yet, here he was mesmerized by Freddie's mouth.

Freddie blinked up at him; his long dark lashes a pretty contrast to his light blue eyes. "Now that your grunting, cave man display is over, what were you saying about Emily?"

"Hold that thought, Drake, can you tell Pepper I need to speak with her, please?"

Drake nodded. "All right. I'll grab her and bring her back." He pressed his hand against TJ's shoulder. "Just stay calm, you hear me?"

TJ met his gaze and nodded.

Drake gave Freddie a one-armed hug before shuffling out the door.

TJ sniffed and glanced around the room, tying to rein in his overwhelming need to rush off with Freddie to somewhere safe—preferably a place with a firm mattress...and lube...and condoms. "Emily, right." He shook his head, refocusing. "Ma called and said I need to come home because Emily's last doctor visit wasn't good. Said something about time being short and all."

Freddie's eyes instantly swelled with tears. He pressed a hand against his mouth before drawing TJ into a hug. "Oh no."

TJ closed his eyes, just taking in this moment with his arms wrapped around Freddie's slim body. Ignoring everything else, he inhaled the soothing scents of lavender coming from Freddie's still slightly damp hair. "In the morning I'll call her doctors to get more detailed info because you know Ma doesn't ever understand what they're saying."

Freddie squeezed him tighter, sniffling a little. "I'm really sorry. Will you tell me what they say?"

TJ eased back then ran the tip of his black Converse High Top across the worn green carpet. "Can you be there when I call?"

Freddie's shoulders slumped. "I'm sorry, I can't. I set up Kyle's first therapy appointment for the morning. Pepper scheduled him with a local doctor, and I-I feel like I should go this first time."

TJ swallowed hard, pressing a hand against his chest, trying to see if his heart had in fact stopped. So this was what they'd come to, Freddie choosing Kyle over him. He knew his thoughts were childish, but they were raw and real, and he couldn't stop the jealousy surging through his blood, coloring this already green room even greener.

Selfishness had always been in his nature. He wanted to be the number one priority in Freddie's life. He wanted friendship, love, and his Dazzler's long legs tangled with his own.

Freddie stepped back, dropping his arms to his sides. "Keep me updated about Emily. I need to get cleaned up and get some sleep." Freddie pressed a kiss against TJ's cheek then squeezed his shoulder like they were just acquaintances or some ridiculous notion like that before he walked away.

Watching him go, TJ blinked back a tear, barely able to breathe or even think, except for one horrid thought—Freddie Davis had just left him for another man.

SIX

Ms. Burris tapped away on her laptop for a moment then stopped and peered over at TJ. "Why didn't you go home right away?"

"Emily's diagnosis was always dire. Until I spoke to the doctors, I wasn't clear on how bad things were. I'd always planned to return to Chicago after the tour, but as you know...those plans changed. It wasn't that I didn't take my Mom's request seriously, only that I never wanted to accept there would actually be an end."

Freddie cleared his throat. "TJ, would you like to take a break?"

"No, I'm okay."

Freddie studied his face for a moment, then seeming to be all right with what he saw, he continued, "To go back to where we are in the story, I'll just say that TJ was right about a lot of things."

"Of course I am."

"No." He held up a finger. "You're right, in that I didn't see the truth about Kyle. I can be a little naïve, because I want to believe people are inherently good, and unfortunately, I had to learn the hard

way to be more cynical. And by the way, you took over the conversa-
tion per usual. So sit back while I talk this time."

FREDDIE TOOK FOUR STEPS TOWARD THE DOOR, AND THEN
stopped and glanced over his shoulder at TJ. The lead singer's black
Apollo concert T-shirt was wrinkled from all the dried sweat and
his head was bent. Freddie closed his eyes and took a deep breath.
Should he leave? Did TJ really need him, or was he just trying to
keep him from Kyle? That look in TJ's eyes though...when Freddie
had walked away, that look had seemed genuinely shocked but he
couldn't trust his judgment where TJ was concerned.

When they were sixteen, he'd finally mustered up the courage
to tell TJ how he felt. They were practicing a song in his basement,
and since Freddie already knew TJ was bisexual, he'd declared his
love and kissed him.

TJ had kissed him back, and for a few months, Freddie had
been in heaven as they'd eased their raging teenage hormones in
every way. But TJ had never said, I love you. Had never made him
promises.

One weekend, their fledgling band had played at a local
college's frat party, and Freddie had stumbled upon TJ in bed with
two college girls. He'd cried for weeks, and after that, he'd never
tried with TJ again. But apparently his heart had never received the
message. And that strong beat in his chest had him wanting to storm
back, grab TJ's face, and kiss away his friend's troubles.

But what his heart hadn't accepted, his mind had always understood. TJ lived for TJ. And Freddie refused to be the lonely-heart-
in-waiting anymore. Sure, he'd be there for TJ since Emily was ill,
but he'd stopped hoping for more on that day he'd seen the love of
his life wrapped around two women.

Heaving a heavy sigh, Freddie took one more look at TJ then

headed to take a shower and swallow down some painkillers for his aching ribs.

He'd never handled conflict well. Maybe that was his problem. Instead of taking the hits, whether emotional or physical, maybe he should find a way to better protect himself. Perhaps he needed counseling, probably so after all he'd endured listening to his father's disapproving words. Just what would his father say if he knew his "pussy-faggot son" was getting hit by his boyfriend?

And what would Freddie do about TJ? If Emily's cancer was in its final stages then TJ would need him more than ever, and Freddie wasn't sure he was strong enough to pull his friend back from the brink. He'd known something was off with their lead singer, because he'd been amazing during their concert. TJ always delivered his strongest performances when he was stressed or hurting. And that rare glimpse into his true self took Freddie's breath away every time.

Freddie brushed a hand down his face and then winced when he touched the bruise. The painful reminder of his own issues served to refocus his mind. Should he give Kyle a chance to change? His dreams of a relationship with TJ would never happen. And if they did, Freddie didn't believe that TJ would remain faithful.

"Stop thinking about that man. Focus on *you* right now," he thumbed his phone, calling Pepper, the band manager. "Hey, Pepper, I need the car to head over to the hotel."

She explained where the car would be so he headed toward the back entrance. The cacophony of sounds around him as everyone broke down after the concert didn't register at all. He'd grown accustomed to the chaos. He was but a speck in the larger machine. Drake and Kim had cornered him earlier, concerned about his bruises. None of his band mates would allow Kyle to remain under Apollo's employ so he'd let the machine continue to spin and would try to keep any further violence from happening between anyone.

After Pepper made Kyle's appointment, he'd done some research on-line. Most male abusers simply believed that men solved problems by fighting or roughhousing. Kyle had said that, too. Somehow Freddie didn't believe that men decided where to eat dinner by shoving each other around first.

Abuse was abuse, whether verbal or physical, and nothing about his current predicament was okay. Plus, the throbbing pain shooting down the side of his face and along his ribcage was a very clear indicator that he was in over his head. Yet this relationship had worked because Kyle was a part of their tour. Finding a partner who didn't want Freddie because of his wealth and status was hard enough, but asking someone to tour with Apollo was a lot to expect from a man.

He really needed a shower. He wanted to hide and cry under the hot spray. He wanted to go home and have his mom make fried chicken and mashed potatoes. But then his father would know his son was in fact a weak girly boy or maybe he'd even say he deserved such a punishment for his sins.

Standing inside the open back door, he waited for Jackson, their driver—a widower with two grown children. Jackson had become a part of their Apollo family five years ago. An absolute professional who kept a lot of Apollo's secrets and was even a good sounding board when Freddie needed a friend.

Freddie stiffened when he heard a familiar whistle. Kyle frequently did that to get his attention over the crowds.

Should he speak to Kyle? Trust that he could get better? Was this what domestic violence victims did? Find excuses for the person who'd beat them bloody?

Kyle stopped at his side, hands in his pockets as he rocked back on his heels. "Hey, you okay?"

"Yes, I'm fine." Freddie stepped back, ready to run.

"I've been thinking a lot about what happened, and I'll get

better for you." He glanced off to the side, rubbing both hands over his face before meeting Freddie's gaze. "I don't know why I can't control my anger."

Freddie shrugged. Good thing they were in public, because merely standing this close to Kyle made his stomach churn. "Okay. I don't know either, but right now, I need to go." He flicked a hand at the waiting black sedan with Jackson at the wheel.

"I'll fix this. I promise." Kyle gently patted his shoulder, before smiling and walking away.

Freddie shivered. Even Kyle's gentle touch repulsed him now.

His gaze traveled across the event space to the green room door. What was back there? His hopes? His dreams? Yeah...and his heart. Poor Kyle had never stood a chance, so shouldn't Freddie give him something? Their relationship was always doomed to end, so he'd try to be a friend while Kyle went through therapy.

Freddie the friend. That's all he'd ever be.

SEVEN

"WOULD ANYONE LIKE COFFEE OR TEA?" FREDDIE GLANCED AT Ms. Burris, who'd been typing away on her tiny laptop for at least an hour now. He'd known this interview would take some time, so he'd had their chef prepare snacks and stock an assortment of beverages. The chef was actually TJ's, at first, and while he'd grumbled at the ridiculousness of having such a luxury, the man did make some amazingly healthy and tasty meals. Having a healthy body was just as important as having a healthy mind.

TJ rose from the couch, and Freddie missed his warmth instantly. "I'll get some drinks. You keep going."

IN THE SEDAN'S BACK SEAT AFTER THE MORNING THERAPY appointment, Freddie fiddled with the unicorn pop-socket on the back of his cell phone. A nervous habit, sometimes he believed these things were invented for anxious people instead of providing a better grip on the phone.

The car's leather seat creaked as Kyle turned to face him. "We'll discuss the appointment in our room."

"You already said you thought she was a quack. You're obviously not willing to listen to what she had to say, so there will be no discussion." He swallowed hard, but continued, "Denial won't work in this instance, Kyle. And to be honest, I don't want to be alone with you again."

"I went to the therapist like you asked. I don't know what else you expect from me."

"Change, that's what I'd like for once. For things to change." Freddie picked at the dark purple polish on his thumbnail. Manicures always relaxed him. He'd have to get another one soon, maybe he'd get blood red this time, as that suited his current mood. RuPaul's gospel number one: *"We're all born naked and the rest is drag."*

"I said I'd try, and I did, Angel. I just think we need our own form of therapy."

Eyes wide, Freddie stared at the beefy hand intruding upon his inner thigh. He stopped the offender and shoved it back on Kyle's side. "No, I don't need anymore of your type of *therapy*." He threw up quotation marks with his fingers. "I'm still bruised from the last round, and I will not be your punching bag again."

Kyle glanced Freddie's way with a sly grin. "I can make things better, Angel. You know I can make you feel good."

Freddie arched a brow, because that was in fact true. Their sex life had been pretty active. His only complaint was that Kyle didn't bottom, while understandable in some relationships, Freddie could see where Kyle used this to assert his dominance. His lover was always very intense during sex, very few soft caresses or slow kisses. "No, Kyle. We had our morning together, and you chose to waste your chance by not listening to the therapist's advice." Freddie glanced out the window, gazing at the bright-green leaves and clear blue sky. "Besides, I need to talk to TJ." Probably not the smartest choice of words since they were alone in the car, which essentially left Freddie a sitting duck.

Kyle ground out, "About what?"

Freddie shrugged, keeping his gaze out the window. His heart had begun beating triple time. *Fear tended to do that to a person.* "His sister. I missed out on his discussion with her doctors because I went with you this morning." There. He'd calmly spoken with none of the shakiness coming through.

"If *I* recall it was your idea to go see that woman, so don't blame me if you didn't get to hear what the doctors said."

"I wasn't blaming you." Freddie countered calmly. "I'm simply explaining what I'm doing today. Not that I owe you any sort of explanation at this point." He breathed in deep, waiting for a hard grip or a strike after that comment. But nothing would keep him from TJ. As promised, he'd accompanied Kyle but that was all he had left to give.

Kyle was quiet for a moment as the car continued on to the hotel. "Are you going to sleep with him?"

Freddie scoffed, finally turning to face Kyle. "Uh...why would you ask that?"

Kyle grunted and shook his head. "He's probably covered in jizz and whatever else after last night's concert anyway."

"Probably." Freddie shrugged, yet hated the visual created with Kyle's words. More so, because they were likely true. They had rocked the hell out of their show last night. Hometown crowds were always insane, and they'd played like they were happy to be home again. TJ was on fire, and Freddie had ripped up the drums as if he were Animal on the Muppets. He loved that crazy, redheaded drummer and even had him tattooed on his right hip.

"I'll come with you." Kyle declared with a nod of his head, as if his words alone had decreed it would happen.

"No, uh, yeah, that's okay." Freddie swallowed hard. "TJ's not real pleased with you right now, and you need to talk to Bruce about your future with his security company anyway. You need to focus on yourself, Kyle. I can't help someone who doesn't want to change." He shrank against the car seat. "That said, TJ's sister is my sister in all ways except blood. Emily's health is what matters to me now. And, no, you don't get to be a part of that. "

Kyle rubbed his forehead. "I don't get you."

"Okay." He drew out the response, sort of a question, sort of an, I'm-fine-with-that as his entire body stiffened. Fear when just conversing with someone was so far from normal. In any relation-ship, he should be able to have a conversation without worrying about a slap to the head or a kick in the ribs.

"I don't understand why you care about TJ or his family. He has shit on you over and over again, and yet, you still moon over him. It's really pathetic, Freddie." Kyle rolled his eyes. "He's not worth your time, and he'll never care about you the way I do. Fuck, you'd probably bend over for him in a minute, but you got me sitting here begging for it."

Freddie breathed a sigh of relief as they drove under the hotel's front portico. Unwilling to continue a conversation that had gone downhill fast, he reached for the door handle before Jackson could get to it. He had to get away from Kyle and his horrid words.

Kyle grabbed his arm. "Is that what you want? Me to beg?"

Freddie didn't turn and caught a glimpse of Jackson rounding the front of the car. Speaking through gritted teeth, he said, "What I want is for you to let me go."

"Fine. I will for now, but we're not done."

Jackson opened the door for Freddie. His brown eyes reflected worry, and he reached across with his freckled, light caramel colored hand to pat Freddie's cheek. "Go on inside now. Old Jackson will take care of everything."

Freddie smiled before stepping out of the car and then went straight to his room. Once inside, he rushed to the bathroom, stripped down, and stood under the hot spray, scrubbing with all his might to wash away the feel of Kyle's touch on his skin.

———

"HEY, FREDDIE?" TJ HOLLERED FROM THE KITCHEN.

"Yeah." He hollered back then turned and winced. "Sorry, Ms. Burris. We're acting like wild animals, yelling across the house like this."

She glanced up from her laptop. "It's okay."

"Fred, could you come here a second?"

"Why?"

"Fred."

"TJ."

"I...uh...I don't know where the coffee is."

Freddie's brow furrowed, because he could literally smell the coffee in the air. He stood and flashed a quick grin to Ms. Burris. "Excuse me."

"Oh, no problem." She stood too, setting her laptop on the coffee table. "I'll just use the restroom."

"Right, it's down the hall and to the left."

She nodded then went left while he went right.

Just as he entered the kitchen, TJ accosted him, pulling him deeper into the kitchen and then into the pantry.

Freddie blinked, eyes adjusting to the dark space. "TJ, what are we doing in here?"

"You're not going to tell her sex stuff, right?"

"Sex stuff?"

TJ braced his palm against Freddie's cheek. "She doesn't need to know sex stuff."

Chuckling, Freddie turned his head and kissed TJ's palm. "I remember how nervous I was going to your room that day. I don't know why, I just was...and then..."

"And then, yeah...but I don't want to share our personal moments with the world, okay?"

Freddie's heart swelled. "Okay. But I'll remember that moment in your hotel room forever."

"Me too, Daz. Me too."

————

FRESHLY SCRUBBED AND SMELLING LIKE A WEST COAST lavender field, Freddie breathed in the calming aroma wafting from his skin while standing outside of TJ's door. Anyone passing by would think he was a weirdo as he'd stood there for at least a full five minutes questioning every decision in his life. "Screw it." He took a deep breath and knocked on the door.

A few moments passed without an answer so he knocked again.

He heard the shuffling of feet then TJ opened the door, rubbing his red-rimmed eyes.

Oh no. The news about Emily must've been really bad because TJ rarely cried. "Hey." Freddie cleared his throat. "Are you... uh...alone?"

"Yeah, come in."

TJ's hair was wet and steam poured out of the bathroom, the scent of pine lingered in the air. Like him, TJ bought expensive beauty products, and he shared his reviews with his zillions of social media followers—*that* part was so not like him. Freddie liked his quiet and his privacy and his drums, maybe a good book or two, and video games. He'd always wished he were smart enough to design those games. *Yeah, him and everyone else aged 25 and under.*

He stepped into the plush gray and white contoured room. Home design was another area of interest and this room was just another boringly decorated space in a hotel that liked to price mini water bottles at five bucks a pop.

Freddie settled into a gray leather chair in the living room area of TJ's suite. "I wanted to come by and talk about Emily. What did the doctors have to say?"

TJ puffed out a breath as he scratched his left shoulder.

Freddie tried not to stare at the outline of TJ's ample package, nestled behind the white boxer briefs. Those thighs though. With the soft brown hair perfectly sprinkled across his muscled legs, Freddie imagined them wrapped around his neck. *Don't!* He would *not* look at the outline of TJ's basically nude body as he stretched his torso to scratch at whatever was still bugging his back.

Lickable. TJ's body was lickable. Hills and valleys, and warmth, and...oh hell...stop! *Close your mouth, no pine scented skin for you!*

He'd zoned out and TJ had been speaking about Emily.

"...it's stage four and nothing can be done. I've known this but...." TJ sighed and flounced onto the black velour couch.

His legs were spread wide, and Freddie had to swallow back a sigh. Setting aside the unwanted and absolutely ridiculous lust flowing under his skin, Freddie flipped on his friend switch. He rose from the chair and sat next to his long-time pal, drawing him close against his shoulder. "What do we need to do?"

TJ hummed out a pleased sound and rested his weight against Freddie. "See that's the thing. It's always been *we* with you."

"Right." Freddie ran a hand along the back of TJ's neck. "It always will be."

"I've been a complete idiot for a long time."

Now wasn't necessarily the time to discuss the long list of TJ's flaws so Freddie went into justification mode. A place he generally found himself when facing TJ's various faults over the years. He had this position down pat. Was a professional even. "You've been enjoying the perks of becoming and being TJ Hardcastle, lead singer of Apollo."

"I don't like him anymore." TJ ran a hand up and down his thigh then drummed his index finger against his knee. "I know I hurt you. I messed us up. But the thing is, with Emily being sick... I'll need you again. I've always needed you, and I know I took you and our friendship for granted, but I promise I won't anymore."

Freddie held back a sigh, because the men in his life were making all these vows and promises and he couldn't bring himself to believe any of it. "I'd do anything for Emily, you know this. And yeah, I've always been right here."

"I know." TJ sat up a little and met his gaze. "But I've made a big mistake."

"What mistake?"

TJ gently cupped Freddie's face. "Not doing more of this."

And then TJ kissed him.

Fireworks exploded in Freddie's body, his heart, and his mind. Clueless as to why this was happening, but for some reason unable to care, Freddie returned the kiss with everything he had.

Their lips gently advanced and retreated in a way that said they had plenty of time. That they would savor and indulge this moment so long in the making. So overdue. So very, very right.

After a long exhalation, TJ grunted out something unintelligible then he gripped Freddie by the back of the neck and angled his head slightly before pressing harder and more urgently. He twisted his tongue along Freddie's, making him moan and want more, so much more.

Freddie eased back when he couldn't catch his breath, which was from either shock or too much pleasure. "Wh-what are you doing? I won't be whatever *this* is for you." He waved a hand between them. "I can't do this again."

"I'm done with the partying. Done playing the game. I miss you, Daz. I have for a long time now." TJ held his gaze for a moment before gently kissing along his non-bruised jawline.

"Well, that's well, th-that's nice...I-I mean..." Freddie pressed a palm against TJ's chest. "Wait. This is all well and good for you, but I don't know that I want whatever this is you're doing. We've already been here and done that."

"We were so young then, Daz. Too young. I needed to live. Be wild. I was so driven, but I got us here, and yeah, I celebrated along the way. I may have left a lot of unforgiveable moments in my wake, but I've always loved you. Always. I know it's unbelievable. I know you'll question the timing, but I won't waver. This thing you're doing with Kyle has always pissed me off. I won't do what he's done, but I *do* want to claim you. I will claim you. Besides,"—TJ winked and lightly kissed his lips—"you love me."

Freddie rubbed his right temple before standing and moving to the other side of the coffee table. He needed something between them before he dropped to his knees and thanked TJ for his final awakening by sucking his dick like a vacuum on steroids. Waving away that stupid visual, he placed both hands on his hips. "What are you talking about? Claiming me? What's wrong with you men lately? I'm not some prize to be won like a stuffed unicorn in some ridiculous carnival stand." Pacing, he threw up his hands and then jabbed a finger at TJ. "Do I love you? Sure, whatever. But I also have this Kyle thing. And there's the Emily thing, and then the whole you're a liar and a cheat and...and I'd never be able to trust you, because you fuck anything that moves, so no. No, no, no! I will not be swayed by your sexy kisses."

TJ grinned and then pressed an open palm against his dick.

"Oh for God's sake, will you stop please?" Freddie rolled his eyes. "You're being stupid."

"First off, you said my kisses were sexy."

"So." Freddie sniffed.

"Second, okay, so we have some trust issues to work out."

"No. I said, no."

"Daz, though I'd rather not talk about Kyle right now. I have to say, he's not worth any further consideration from you. I don't like being lumped into all of his shit either. I mean, *I* never hit you."

"No, you've just *broken my heart*." Freddie yelled the last few words and kicked the table but only managed to hurt his big toe and knock TJ's game controller onto the floor. Ignoring the pain, he forged on, "I've been trying to reach you for years. Every song I've written was ripped from my heart, but you never heard. You never listened."

"Fuck you for that." TJ growled back, pointing his own accusing finger. "I *do* hear. Every word. And it's because I do, that I sing my heart out." He took a deep breath. "I've always felt it, too, but I wasn't ready. If I'd given in to what we felt for each other before, I likely would've hurt you so much more."

"Bull crap. You haven't said anything about wanting me, not to mention all the men...and women...and men."

"I couldn't stop. Okay?" TJ raked a hand through his damp strands. "Once we hit it big, I couldn't stop, and I don't know if I can apologize for that because I needed it, not...not as much as I needed you, but dang it..." He shook his head. "I have it all now when before I had nothing. Give me a break for enjoying the things I never had."

"No. No breaks." Freddie slashed a hand through the air. "I gave you *years*."

"I know. I wanted everything for the both of us so I gave up everything to establish the band. But the band's set now. I can stop.

I can breathe, and now that I can breathe, I want to breathe with you."

Oh holy smokes, that was good. So convincing, and sweet and lovely and every word Freddie had longed to hear for so long. But he had to remain strong, because wasn't he suffering even now from Kyle's manipulative words? Wasn't TJ doing the same? Using words to persuade him? Saying things he thought Freddie wanted to hear? *No!*

He'd steel his heart because the poor organ still held scars from all the times he'd let himself dream of really and truly loving TJ Hardcastle. "I'm glad you think you get to make all the decisions about how we'll move forward in our relationship, TJ."

"As I said, if I'd tried this before, I would've ruined everything. I kept you at a distance because—"

"Because you're selfish."

"I am. Yes." TJ tapped a finger against his bottom lip. "So you'd rather settle for somebody who beats you? Fuck that, Freddie. I might not be a prize but I care, and I will never hit you."

Freddie refused to acknowledge the slight wiggle of hope trying to force its way up to his brain in order to redirect all the synapses that already had assigned TJ to the never-ever zone. He also refused to acknowledge the surge of desire firing along his skin as TJ lounged with his legs spread. And no way did he note the dark trail leading straight to a very impressive cock that at this moment looked rather needy. "I don't have any idea what to say to you right now except I don't believe you."

"Write how you feel in a song then. Say it with lyrics like you always do, and I'll sing it. Yours fears will be gone then. I'll make it escape through my lungs and out my mouth. It'll fly up into the rafters and sail away."

"You're not the wordsmith in this relationship, so shut up, and besides maybe *I'd* like to sing it."

"I wish you would. We both know you belong behind a mic."

"I don't have your..." Freddie flicked a hand toward the lead singer's body then shrugged.

"My what?" TJ arched a brow and gripped his obviously hard dick through his now taut briefs.

Freddie inhaled deeply and tried to pretend that the arousal floating through the air didn't have a heady smell and that it didn't smell like his all-consuming need for TJ. He avoided noting the wet imprint of pre-cum on TJ's briefs, and he for sure didn't lick his lips, thinking about that warm flavor on his tongue.

He swallowed hard and then sank back into the gray chair. "I don't like writing songs about how much I miss you. I don't *want* to want things that are bad for me. I'm messed up, TJ. I'm with a guy who hits me, and I need to fix things. Fix *me*. I can't do this with you right now. I'm an emotional wreck and trying to figure out your motives will do me in. I'm sorry. I'm just so scared of everything and...and I hate it." He pounded a fist on the chair's arm before wiping a tear off his cheek. "I hate it," he whispered, staring at the light gray carpet, willing away the tears.

TJ knelt between Freddie's legs and tipped up his chin. "Look at me."

Shaking his head, Freddie stared at the artwork mounted across the wall. Not a lighthouse this time, but instead black and white slashes, which just hurt his head, because he liked living in the gray. Life wasn't black and white. But maybe he should be more final in his thoughts, just go all black. No, he was blond with blue eyes, black had never been his color. He sighed. *Wow, avoidance much, Dazzler?* He focused on TJ's chin instead of those brown eyes that would suck away all resistance. After sighing, he said, "I just asked you to let me figure out my life, and you're on your knees blocking me in." He frowned and shook his head. "Why won't anyone listen to me?"

"Daz, just close your eyes for a second."

"What? Why?"

"Just close your eyes."

He did.

"Breathe in with me, Freddie."

He did.

"Breathe out."

He didn't.

Instead Freddie opened his eyes and fastened his mouth to those plump lips, waiting directly across from his own. No willpower. None. And likely very stupid, but that hope signal had finally zapped across his brain, and TJ was between his legs so who could blame him?

TJ returned the kiss by angling his head and brushing his tongue across Freddie's. Groaning, TJ gripped his hips and yanked him forward.

Freddie hissed. "Ow."

"What?" TJ lifted both hands at his sides, his lips wet and burnished red. "What happened?"

The pain in Freddie's side served as a very serious reminder that his life was a big ole mess right now. "What happened is that I was reminded of how much I hurt."

TJ opened his mouth.

"No." Freddie pressed a finger against those soft lips. "I need to break away from Kyle for good, and I'll admit he's not taking that well. And you need my friendship to get through this tough time with Emily." He sighed again and glanced at his Apple watch as it buzzed with a call from Drake. "If you mean what you've said, you'll be my friend for now...and then...if you want more, and *I'm* willing for more, then we'll see."

TJ kept his gaze for a moment before nodding. "Okay, I agree." He stood and pulled Freddie to his feet.

Without another word, TJ led Freddie to the room's entryway. Placing a hand against the door, he ran his free hand down the back of Freddie's neck and then squeezed, brushing his thumb against the fine hairs, making him shiver. "Remember when we used to catch fireflies and put them in those soup cans. We'd poke holes in the sides, and you'd always let them go because you were worried their friends and family would miss them?"

"Well, we *were* essentially kidnapping them."

TJ laughed before crossing both arms against his chest and leaning on the wall by the door. "I remember one time you were letting a bunch go, and I just watched you. We were like thirteen, I think. I had already started to see you differently, and you were talking to those bugs telling them to fly home. And I remember thinking, *he's* become my home. My life was major shit back then, but I had you and that was important. I think I shoved you and gave you hell for being a sap, but that's just how we were. Even then, I knew we'd get here someday. In the dark. With the fireflies, because you've always been my light."

Freddie's jaw dropped. "Wow." He started slow clapping. "That was nice. Very nice. You keep up that sweet talk, Hardcastle, and maybe we'll get somewhere."

"That *was* pretty epic." TJ glanced back at the living room. Likely wondering where he'd put his phone.

Freddie rolled his eyes. "Good gravy, do *not* post any of that on social media."

"First off, stop saying good gravy. You're not eighty years old, sitting on the front porch of some retirement home in a wooden rocker." He grinned and shook his head. "And secondly, my fans need to hear my love moment."

"I'm leaving now." Freddie opened the hotel room's door. "Maybe you'll find me frolicking through a field of fireflies, glowing as your light or whatever." With his own cocky grin, and ignoring

TJ's curses, Freddie quickly shut the door and laughed all the way back to his room. *Huh?* This happy glow in his chest was pretty awesome, but Freddie had his doubts it would last. But what if it did? What if they could shine together they way he'd always dreamed they would? He clutched a hand to his chest, holding in TJ's words because that "love moment" was the most beautiful thing Freddie had ever heard.

EIGHT

"So we were at the part where I left Kyle in the hotel." Settled back in the living room, Freddie glanced at Ms. Burris while clenching his right hand into a fist. It still ached a little, maybe real, maybe imagined, but never faded. "This next part might be hard to hear." Freddie leaned back against the couch, running a finger along the rim of his steaming coffee cup. "You probably heard about my hand."

"I did, yes."

"What you don't know, but what I want others to understand is that I get it. The absolute fear around your abuser and just how much pain they can and do inflict."

"That's why I'm here."

"Okay, yeah, let's get through this then."

Song lyrics—and maybe a few fireflies—buzzing through his head, Freddie practically floated back to his room. He pressed two fingers against his lips, relishing the memory of TJ's kisses.

A bit before lunch, he wrapped a hand around his waist when his stomach grumbled. The loud gurgle was the only sound aside from a soda machine's hum. Once he got settled in his room, he'd fire up his laptop and write like he always did, pouring out his innermost emotions. Sometimes those words became songs, and sometimes he just left the words on paper, unwilling to share too much of himself with Apollo's fans or anyone else for that matter. After he spilled all the words in his head, he'd text TJ to discuss the plans regarding Emily. He'd gone there to talk about her, but TJ's kisses had distracted him from his purpose.

Licking his lips, he tasted TJ again and couldn't help but wonder what would happen if he did believe that his friend could actually change? What if they got together and everything fell apart? What would happen to Apollo then? Could they take that chance? And shouldn't he take some time to consider how his relationship with Kyle had turned so violent? So twisted and wrong? But hadn't all the men in his life hurt him? His father? TJ? And now Kyle simply added to that list.

Sighing, he shoved the key card into the slot. The button turned green, and the card reader beeped. He shoved open the door and stepped inside.

Darkness.

Pulse racing, he blinked. Had he shut all the blinds? Maybe the cleaning lady had shut them. But then why was his fight or flight kicking in as he glanced around the too dark and too quiet room?

"Where have you been?"

That voice. So calm yet deep and filled with accusation.

A wave of dizziness crashed over Freddie, weakening his knees, and he stumbled a step further into the room. "H-how d-did you get in here?" He jumped as the door clicked shut behind him.

"I'm band security. I have keys to all your rooms."

"I'd like you to leave." Freddie swallowed hard and groped behind him for the door handle.

A primal roar came from the dark before Kyle's form appeared, like some horror movie madman, wielding a chainsaw or bloody blade but this man only needed his fist.

"Where the fuck have you been?" Kyle shoved Freddie against the door, pressing his hand against the drummer's throat.

Gasping for air, Freddie kicked and tried prying Kyle's hand free.

Kyle gripped the longer hair at the top of Freddie's head and dragged him across the room before tossing him to the floor. "I said, where have you been? I've been waiting for you for an hour!"

Hand against his aching throat, Freddie scooted back against the wall, and drew his entire body in tight, making himself a smaller target. "I-I told you I went to talk to TJ."

"Always him. Never me. Never us." Kyle paced back in forth in front of him. "Everything is always about TJ."

"Kyle, p-please." Freddie lifted a hand between them even while facing the harsh reality that nothing he said would change what was to come. He'd be beaten, likely worse than ever before. And he was too weak to stop it. Cold fear shot down his spine and landed in his stomach which stirred up a huge pot of bile that threatened to expel all over Kyle's heavy brown boots. "Listen, please. Think about what you're doing. Remember what the therapist said, step back and remain calm." Rising on his knees, Freddie searched Kyle's eyes, but the man's lack of empathy was more than evident in his hard gaze.

"Shut up about that quack bitch. I did that *for you*. I do what *you* ask and where does that get me?" Kyle threw both hands up. "A begging fool. That's what I am. Begging for scraps of your attention. Scraps of your love. I've never meant anything to you. You're always off with TJ and your band, leaving me behind. The therapist can't say shit about that. She doesn't know me. What I put up with day in and day out. How much you tease me. You think I'm a fool. You flaunt yourself in front of all those fans and in front of TJ, well I won't have it. You're mine."

Skin clammy, Freddie rubbed his shaking hands against his thighs and glanced at the door. Could he make it? He scrabbled to his feet, easing along the wall, barely breathing and in denial about how far he could actually travel before he was knocked to the ground again. *Dirt, disinfectant, and cum.* That's where he'd end up again. That thought had him glancing at the ranting man before him. Kyle's face was a deep red and spittle flew from his lips with each word. His jaw clenched tight and his body wired to strike.

But then Kyle stopped.

"Wait, wait, wait." He held up an index finger. "If you didn't have this band then…then you could be with me." His eyes went wide, and he stuck out his hand. "Come here."

"N-no. G-get away from me." Cringing, Freddie inched another step toward the door, all while curling both arms against his sides in anticipation of the heavy blows from Kyle's fists.

"I said, come here!"

Oh, please no! Freddie felt as if he couldn't breathe yet at the same time, he was rasping out each breath like he'd run a marathon. He glanced at Kyle, then at the door, and then back at Kyle again.

"Don't you do it."

He shot toward the door.

Strong arms banded around his shoulders, spinning him around before shoving him to the floor.

Freddie bounced against the wall, scrambled for purchase but lost his footing and landed on his back.

Kyle dropped to his knees, placing them on each side of Freddie's body.

With a whimper, Freddie braced his arms in front of his face.

Kyle shoved them aside, bent, and then kissed him. Hard.

Twisting, Freddie struggled to break free, slapping at Kyle's head, and trying to buck him off. His elbow smarted after he banged it against the unforgiving floor.

"Stop, Angel." Sweat dripping off his face, Kyle captured both of Freddie's hands in one of his and slammed them above the drummer's head.

Grunting, Kyle kissed him again, wetter, sloppier, and sucking on Freddie's tongue.

The kiss tasted like stale beer. And anger and hate. And everything Freddie hated in the world. He tried to bite and turn away but Kyle only followed, forcing him to accept his unwanted attentions.

"Feisty little thing, aren't you?"

Kyle's hard erection pressed against Freddie's hip.

No! Oh God, no. Being beaten was one thing but if Kyle raped him, what then? Who would he become? *What* would he become? Broken. Damaged. Destroyed. Ripped in two and the "weak bitch" his father had always claimed him to be. He'd never be able to face anyone again due to the degradation. How did someone survive such a thing?

"No!" Tears pouring down his cheeks, Freddie squirmed against Kyle's greater bulk. "Get off me."

Kyle simply shook his head. "I'll make you mine. All mine."

Freddie froze, and even his heart seemed to halt, afraid to make a sound. What did that mean? *Make you mine?* What would Kyle do? "Please, don't do this." He wanted to shout, scream until someone heard him, but his words were barely above a whisper.

His tormentor brought Freddie's right hand to his lips then sucked his index finger into this hot, disgusting mouth. "I have to do this Freddie. It's the only way."

"What?" Freddie swore that every hair on the back of his neck lifted. "What way? What do you mean?"

Kyle ran his fingers along the inside of Freddie's open right palm. "This hand. This is how I'll win you. This will set you free."

"What will set me..."

Kyle bent his index finger all the way back until a crack sounded in the otherwise quiet room.

"Holy mother fucker!" Freddie struggled to pull away as searing pain shot through his hand and up his arm, kicking starting his heart again. "S-stop, just stop. I'll do whatever, please." Tears poured down his face. Bile rising from the pain. "N-not my hand. P-please not my hand."

"It's the only way." Kyle shook his head before yanking back Freddie's pinky finger.

"Oh, my God, please no!"

A soft snap joined the sound of Kyle's odd, almost a manic-giggle.

Freddie screamed. He cursed. He begged and pleaded, trying to break free from Kyle's hard grip.

A loud rumble ripped from the depths of his soul as Kyle gripped his thumb and bent it back until it popped.

Every pain receptor in Freddie's body reacted to the sound, and he entered a zone where his blood turned to fire, burning through his veins like a feral creature slicing him open from the inside.

Sobs joined with screams and curses and words that made no sense. He couldn't break free and couldn't save himself from whatever Kyle decided to deliver. Would he die now? Was his hand only the beginning?

Kyle held him tight in his arms, rocking him back and forth. "It's all right now, Angel. I've got you. We'll be all right. I promise."

Soft words continued to buzz through his ear, but he blocked them.

The agony, overbearing and raw was the only sound he heard now—a whooshing of blood racing through his veins, sending pain in every direction. He gasped as he lifted his hand to his face.

His fingers...oh God, his fingers.

He swallowed hard and closed his eyes, trying to block out the picture of his fingers bent in an unnatural manner.

His livelihood destroyed in minutes.

Kyle had finally taken everything.

His hands were his life.

His drums were his life.

No hands meant no drums.

Dazed, he opened his eyes and pressed his broken fingers against Kyle's chest, hoping the excruciating throbbing would pound hard enough to knock him out. A stinging sensation flowed from the broken places until he gasped. But it wasn't enough to reach that black out—to find release and escape the pain.

Furious and beyond caring what happened next, he punched Kyle's chest over and over with his broken hand. "Take it all. Just take it." He cried and screamed but darkness didn't come—and neither did Kyle's rage.

His ex-lover simply gripped Freddie's flailing arms before throwing him over his shoulder and then tossing him on the bathroom floor

Holding his mangled hand against his chest, Freddie gazed up at the monster before him.

Kyle smiled a twisted smile and said two words. Two words that scared Freddie more than anything had before. Two words that were spoken in a tone so sure, so determined that even Freddie believed they were true. Two words that sent shivers along his spine and would haunt him for the rest of his life.

"You're mine."

NINE

TJ held a sobbing Freddie against his chest. "It's okay now, Daz."

Shaking his head and mumbling something about his gross nose, Freddie turned to Ms. Burris and excused himself.

TJ offered the reporter a weak smile then glanced in Freddie's direction, knowing if he followed the love of his life, he'd spend the rest of the day comforting him. Yet, Freddie didn't want that, so he continued on...

After Freddie walked out his hotel room, TJ had relieved his aching dick with a tight grip and a ton of tissues. The release had hit fast and hard as thoughts of his drummer's kiss swirled through his head. Yet, the orgasm wasn't quite as satisfying without the actual man beside him, stroking him, and bringing him to satisfaction.

Once he'd taken care of his overwhelming need—and washed his hands, he'd called his sister, Emily.

After the call, he'd crumpled onto the edge of the couch and let his arms swing freely between his legs. With too many feelings ricocheting through his mind, he tossed his phone onto the coffee table and wiped away the tears streaming down his face. How gross would it be if he used one of the tissues on the floor?

He picked up one then grimaced. Rising to his feet, he frowned when his knees cracked and popped like rice krispies in a cold bowl of milk. He tore off all his clothing and headed for the bathroom. His state of mind had gone from happy and horny to devastated and helpless. He'd hop in the shower and lose his shit for a few minutes before gathering the band together to break the news that they were done with the tour. *Fuck!* It'd be a public relations nightmare, but he didn't care. Not after he'd heard the hopelessness in his sister's voice after she'd repeated everything her doctors' had said.

He swallowed hard as he flicked on the sink's hot water and washed his hands. Drying his hands on the soft white towel, he glanced in the mirror and stuck out his tongue at the guy with red-rimmed eyes and a red-tipped nose. "Your family and your band need you strong. We'll figure something out for Emily. I won't let her..." He wouldn't say the d-word. Wouldn't and couldn't. "I won't let her go. I can do this. They need me. Freddie needs me. I'm not giving up yet." Jaw clenched, he turned and flipped on the shower.

One word existed that he hated above all others: metastatic. They'd always known his sister was terminal—metastatic or whatever. Breast cancer that spread into her lungs, bones, and every other place the cells decided to create chaos. Sure she'd lived for four years after her diagnosis, but treatment could only keep her alive for so long. Sometimes, she'd feel okay but then she'd go to the grocery store and have to rest for three days. Her inactivity had increased lately. He should've seen the signs but he'd been living in his own world, thinking his money could save her. If he just kept going, making more, he could use it to find a cure. Hell, he'd donated thousands to research. What the hell were they doing with it all?

When Apollo hit it big right after her diagnosis, she'd smiled and told him to grab life by the balls and live. Live for her and live his dream. She'd demanded he send her pictures and videos of his adventures and so he did. Sure, he shared most of his life on social media, but the real moments were only for her. Before his first concert, he'd been a mess until he'd video messaged her and blurted all his fears. She'd eased his mind and made him remember his purpose. Though not beside him physically, he'd taken her everywhere. She was his number one fan, and he hated to consider living without her.

His phone rang on the sink's counter top. He stared at it, unsure how it'd gotten there. Must've grabbed it on his way to the bathroom—didn't all his friends say it was an extension of his hand anyway?

Drake's ring tone stopped then started up again.

Steam filled the bathroom and he considered ignoring the call, but then Drake rang again.

He hit the speakerphone button. "What?"

"Where are you? I've been pounding on your door for like an hour."

TJ rolled his eyes. "I'm jumping in the shower. What do you want?"

"I want you to answer the door."

TJ growled out a curse as he stared at the disconnected call. He flicked off the water, which had likely reached the optimal temperature, and sighed. "This better be good. I needed some serious water therapy, but no, I gotta answer the stupid door to Drake's stupid face." After grumbling to himself, he headed for the door and then realized he was completely naked—and not just his body. His soul was shaken and everything he was feeling was evident in his bright red eyes and beet-red nose. Running a hand over his face, he turned on his heel and then shouted over his shoulder. "Give me a minute!"

Grabbing a pair of workout pants from his haphazardly packed suitcase, he ignored Drake's ring tone piercing the silence of his room. Again. And headed for the door. Again. Whipping it open, he glared at his lead guitarist. "What the hell, man?"

Drake barreled past him into the room then stopped and faced him, hands locked on his hips. "We have to cancel the tour."

TJ blinked then shoved the door with his heel. It shut with a soft click. "I'm sorry, what did you say?"

Drake raked his fingers through his shoulder-length curly, blond hair. "So...um...like, okay, just listen and don't freak out." He held up a hand. "Okay?"

TJ's stomach dropped. This was bad, so bad. And after dealing with Freddie and their firefly-moment and then his nightmare-inducing phone call with Emily, he wasn't sure how much more he could take. *He* was the one planning to cancel the tour, so had Drake somehow heard from Emily? "Drake, this day has been shit, like major hell fire shit, so spit out why *you* think we're cancelling."

Drake opened his mouth then closed it. Then he stepped forward and placed a hand on TJ's shoulder. "All right. So, about an hour ago, I knocked on Freddie's door and he wouldn't answer. We were supposed to go over some timing on that new piece he'd written. I mean, he's the one that scheduled the time, and you know he's serious about his schedule."

TJ nodded and waved his hand in a circle. "Right, right. Go on."

"Well, I'm starting to get a little pissed, cause Kim wanted to play the new *God of War* game but then Kyle answers the door and wouldn't let me in."

"Is that right?" TJ shrugged off Drake's hold and crossed both arms over his chest.

"Yeah, I knew something was off because Freddie doesn't cancel, right, so when he wouldn't answer his phone, I found Bruce. He went off, man. He calls the hotel manager, has him unlock the door, and...and..." Drake heaved in a deep breath and bit his bottom lip.

TJ glanced around for his shoes. He had an ass to kick. "Spit it out. What did Kyle do?" He spotted his slides and even knowing they wouldn't do much damage to Kyle's ass, he slid them on and rounded on Drake. "Where is he?"

"Freddie was in the bathroom, man."

"No, damn it. Not Freddie. Where. Is. Kyle?" Rage flowing through his veins, he stomped toward the door.

Drake's eyes went wide. "No, TJ. Stop! Freddie needs you right now. Not violence. Not shouts. Not anything loud. Okay?" He shot forward and gripped TJ's hand before he could open the door. "Listen, this is really bad. So calm down and just listen. Please."

"Bad. It's *bad*? Of course it's bad." TJ threw both hands in the air, before punching the wall. "Fuck!"

"Oh, great." Drake yanked TJ's hand closer.

A drip of blood blossomed on his index finger's knuckle.

"Just what we need, two broken band mates."

"What?" TJ sucked the blood off his hand. It wasn't broken so what the hell was Drake talking about?

Drake met his gaze and then swallowed visibly. "Freddie was just lying on the bathroom floor and well, I-I didn't know what to do. He was crying and all crumpled up. And Bruce was yelling. And Kyle wouldn't leave." Drake bent over and braced his hands just above his knees. Shaking his head, he straightened and then ran a hand over his mouth. "I'd never seen anything like it...but we have cancel the tour because Kyle broke three of Freddie's fingers. And

Kim and I already decided that we don't want a replacement. We won't play without Fred."

TJ just stared at Drake, not computing everything his band mate had spit out like a rapid-fire machine gun. "Wait, Freddie was lying on the floor? Of the bathroom?" TJ breathed in deeply through his nose, trying to string everything together. "Three fingers? Broken?"

"Right, we found Freddie on the bathroom floor. Kyle broke three fingers on his right hand."

"His right hand." TJ braced his own hand against the wall. "But h-he needs his hand."

"Yeah, he does." Drake stepped toward the door. "I've called for the car, and Bruce is dealing with everything and everyone else. Jared is handling your schedule so come with me. Freddie needs us at the hospital."

"Oh God, Drake." TJ sucked in a breath as everything finally became clear. "Out of all the things Kyle could do to Fred, he had to take his hand?"

"I know." Drake nodded and then drew him into a hug.

TJ blinked. His entire body had gone cold at the thought of Freddie alone, scared, and broken on a bathroom floor. The terror his friend must've endured was unimaginable. He'd fix this. He'd let Freddie handle the Kyle situation on his own but that was over, right now.

TJ clutched Drake by the shoulders, easing him away while keeping his gaze. "This ends now. I don't care what Freddie wants, says, or does. His safety is paramount. Kyle will be arrested for assault. There will be restraining orders and repercussions. I'm finished with all this, but-he-just-needs-therapy stuff. Tried it, and it didn't work. I don't care what our lawyer's say, what Pepper says, or what our public relations team says. Kyle is facing the music on this. This is the third time he's hurt Freddie, and that's one time too many." He took a deep breath. "I'm trying to remain calm about this, but if anyone tries to stop me from ending Kyle, I will go all rock star on their ass, you with me?"

Drake nodded. "I'm with you. Kim's with you. Freddie might not feel like he has any power, but he does. We do. And we'll wield it. I'm behind you one-hundred percent."

With no shirt—or fucks left to give, TJ whipped open the door and barreled down the hall. Phone in hand, he thumbed through his contacts. Behind him, he could hear Drake speaking to someone on his phone, likely Kim.

His first call would be to Bruce, Kyle's boss, because apparently the man didn't quite understand the definition of the word security.

———

WITH A SHAKY LEFT HAND, FREDDIE TUGGED THE THIN hospital blanket closer to his chest. Humiliation still lingered from Drake and Bruce storming into his hotel room and finding him a blubbering mess on the bathroom floor.

It'd taken four men to drag a kicking and screaming Kyle from the room, his face bright red as threats poured from his mouth.

Half of *his* face was now buried in the lumpy pillow that smelled a little like bleach, Freddie couldn't even care enough to wipe the tears slowly leaking down his face or wipe his dripping nose.

He shivered. His blood was too busy pounding in his hand to be heating the rest of his body. Or maybe the hospital liked freezing their patients to death? Who knew and who cared?

His hand was destroyed.

His life was over.

Sure, they said his fingers would heal, but would they?

He was nothing without his drums.

The band could go on without him. Leave him behind like he deserved for dragging them through this mess.

No one wanted a broken and bruised fool.

A familiar voice reverberated from the hallway into his room. TJ being his usual obnoxious self with shouts and threats. And Drake's more soothing tone, likely trying to calm TJ down.

Freddie closed his eyes. Maybe if he couldn't see them, they couldn't see him. A fruitless hope. Especially since Kim was already sitting in the room and had given him her thoughts in her normal no-nonsense manner. He'd likely hear the same from TJ though in a much more colorful way. They'd try to take over his life, but hell, he wasn't doing such a good job anyway.

TJ stormed into the room.

Of course, Freddie didn't know this for sure as he kept his eyes shut, faking sleep. Yet, he was right because the door banged against the wall, making him jump.

Freddie heard someone gasp then TJ said, "I'll kill him."

Drake said, "Let's just keep our cool."

Kim said, "Freddie's asleep so shut up."

The drugs were working their magic, because even if Freddie wanted to open his eyes, he doubted he could.

TJ's warm fingers brushed through his hair. "What did he do to you?"

Freddie couldn't stand the pain evident in TJ's voice so he cracked open his eyelids, but couldn't think of a word to say. The loud sob that ripped from his throat said everything he couldn't.

Shirtless and wearing low-slung work out pants, TJ bent and pressed his forehead against Freddie's "Oh, Daz. He got you good. I never should've listened to you. Never again. You hear me."

"TJ, he doesn't need I told you so's right now." Kim rose from her chair and wrapped her slim arm around TJ's waist. "Although, I see you finally got your head out of your ass and caught on to what's been in front of you all along." Kim pointed to the tissue box. "Get him some tissues, Drake."

Drake handed TJ the box.

TJ pulled a few free and gently wiped Freddie's cheeks and nose. "We'll get through this. Don't worry about anything. We'll handle it all. You just get some rest."

Freddie chewed his bottom lip, and almost whimpered when TJ pulled away. He'd needed the warmth, the security. Meeting TJ's eyes, he considered his lead singer's words. Wouldn't that be nice, letting everyone take care of his problems? But was that the right choice? How could he ever become strong if he let others gently pull him along? Yet with his broken fingers cradled against his chest, he wondered if he knew the right path anymore. His entire body was still locked in fear and his livelihood was in question. Figuring out life decisions while still in shock wasn't such a great idea. He'd need quiet and space, and time, and a safe place to just think through everything. A place that didn't hurt and didn't have a thundering man in heavy boots, breaking off little pieces of his sanity—and his body. His world was out of rhythm and he had no idea how to find a steady beat again. "I appreciate you guys being here. I'm not ready to talk though."

"Freddie, we—"

"No, TJ, just please, give me some quiet. I can't think right now."

"We need to make some decisions."

Freddie swallowed hard. "I understand."

TJ narrowed his brow. "Understand what? Because I didn't say anything yet."

A tear slipped down Freddie's cheek, and Kim leaned over and wiped it away.

"Fred, it'll be okay. We stick together, so whatever is going through that head of yours, stop." Kim's brown eyes were soft, tears forming at the edges but then she turned to TJ and glared. "You stop, too. He asked for space, so give it."

TJ opened his mouth, with what would've been regrettable words, but luckily a nurse sauntered into the room, wearing a bright pink top with green, pink, and yellow owls printed on the fabric.

"You're good to go, Mr. Davis." She glanced at him then came to an abrupt stop when she caught sight of TJ. "Oh...well, oh, you're TJ Hardcastle."

Her hand came up to cover her mouth. Freddie rolled his eyes. Some things never changed. Kim had been in the room all this time, but this nurse just now realized who they were. He sighed and met Kim's gaze. She shook her head, which made him smile.

TJ nodded his hello but waved a hand at Freddie. "Thank you for taking care of him. We'll get him home. Tell me what we need to do."

The nurse smiled, her cheeks turning pink but she gave a thorough list of his care.

His care. Freddie scoffed and stared at his worthless hand.

He should've insured each finger.

But that insurance wouldn't keep Kyle from hunting him down. His ex was becoming one of those obsessed stalkers that would kill him if they couldn't be together. A nightmare. A made-for-TV-movie on the Investigation Discovery channel.

He shivered while recalling Kyle's ominous words. *"You're mine."*

"You cold, Freddie?" Drake frowned as he stepped closer.

Freddie shrugged. "Yeah. It's cold in here. Why isn't TJ wearing a shirt?" Not only was the lead singer shirtless, but he was wearing Nike slides with no socks. This whole situation was surreal, and he just wanted to hide under a warm, fluffy blanket with fifteen levels of security guarding him as he slept.

As it was, he let Drake's explanation flow over him. Let the nurse continue talking to TJ and Kim. But those two words remained at the forefront of his mind. *"You're mine."*

Those words were not true. They weren't. They couldn't be, but Freddie knew it'd be a long time before his new pal—soul deep fear—left his side. With a broken right hand, he wasn't *free* to do anything. Wasn't free to write. Wasn't free to release all his pent-up aggression on the drums. Wasn't free at all.

TEN

"Wow, THE REPORTS SAID FREDDIE BROKE HIS FINGERS, BUT hadn't mentioned all that." Ms. Burris glanced at Freddie with sympathy in her eyes.

Taking a moment to remember he was safe now and that his hand had healed, Freddie glanced out the windows, noting the shadows created by the outdoor furniture. They'd need lunch soon. He sighed and faced the reporter again. "It was brutal, yeah. Cancelling all those tour stops was like trying to stop a speeding train only knowing there's nothing you can do. You just have to sit back and watch it crash into a mountain or whatever. I don't know, but yeah, that wasn't a good time for our band or our fans."

TJ placed a hand on Freddie's knee and squeezed. "We did what we had to do."

Freddie nodded. "We did."

TJ stretched, popping his back. "Ready to move on?"

Freddie nodded then his cheeks heated because he remembered TJ's request for no "sex stuff" and considering where they were in the story, he'd have to be sure to skip over as much as he could.

. . .

PEPPER HAD REBOOKED THEIR DOWNTOWN CHICAGO HOTEL rooms for a couple more nights since they couldn't move on to Indianapolis for the next tour stop. Freddie had stayed in the room all afternoon while the band dealt with the logistics and issues of postponing the tour. After returning from the hospital, Bruce had brought by a policeman. Freddie had recalled his attack, and then the cop had taken a few pictures of his bruised body.

Now, early evening, Freddie sprawled on the hotel room's bed and lifted his hand before his face. His index finger and pinky were in splints and attached to the finger beside it with tape, as if in a permanent Vulcan salute. His thumb was off on its own. They'd worried his pinky would require surgery but that hadn't been the case. The whole situation upset his stomach and made him want to curl up in a ball and watch reruns of *RuPaul's Drag Race* while inhaling orange sherbet by the bucket.

Freddie stretched out his legs and sighed, glad he'd decided to room with TJ rather than going back to where he'd been a victim of Kyle's insanity.

He glanced across the king-sized bed at a shirtless TJ who'd come back about an hour ago, showered, and then plopped on the bed beside him before he'd turned on the Xbox and started playing *God of War*. "Who was at the door earlier?"

"Jared."

Freddie grunted in reply. Full of anger, resentment, and residual fear on top of being pissed that he was still scared added a whole dollop of surliness to his attitude. Plus if TJ's phone didn't quit pinging with text messages and calls, he'd throw the stupid thing out the window. When it pinged again, he gritted his teeth. "Do you think you could silence your phone, please?"

TJ paused his game and then glanced at the text. "Sorry, no.

Jared's handling what he can so I can be here with you, but he still likes to check with me."

"I never said I needed a baby sitter," Freddie grumbled.

TJ kept his gaze on his phone as his fingers flew across the screen.

"Why not just keep the tour going without me?"

TJ kept typing on his phone as he said, "We won't continue without you, and I need to spend time with Emily. I actually need to get over there tonight."

"Well, I'm not stopping you."

TJ tossed his phone on the side table. "Yeah, you kind of are. Not to mention, I had a lot of work to oversee this afternoon. The entire team has been busting their butts to accommodate us."

"I'm aware of this, TJ." Freddie rolled his eyes. Better to be irritated than let the guilt wash through him. Being alone wasn't really in the cards right now, and he hated that jump in his stomach every time someone knocked on the door. TJ had said Drake and Kim were handling a lot, as well, which made him feel even worse as he hadn't even wanted to look at his phone. "TJ."

"Yeah." He glanced over his shoulder from where he'd been customizing the armor for Kratos.

"I just wanted to say thank you and stuff."

"Okay." He grinned. "You're welcome and stuff."

Freddie sighed. "I'm being completely unprofessional right now, and I have no idea where my phone is to even handle anything."

"Kim has it."

"What?"

"I gave it to Kim and told her to do what she could and to give the rest to Pepper. We pay our team a boat load of money so they can help us out on this one."

"Kim has my phone?"

"Yes."

"Great. Just great." He hadn't even thought about it before, but now he felt like his third arm was missing. Phone addiction was a real thing, not a TJ-level thing, but real enough all the same.

TJ halted the game again and turned, biting his bottom lip. "So...Drake said things were pretty messed up when he found you in the bathroom."

Freddie's chest tightened, and he picked at a stray string on the beige blanket. "Yeah. Kyle, he...he was...I'd rather not talk about Kyle right now." He hadn't quite accomplished locking away the pain and utter fear and added to that was the memory of Kyle's manic giggle, which replayed on a loop in his head.

"Fred, you should talk about it."

"Yeah, probably, but I'm not ready. I have a lot..." he waved a hand in a circle by his chest. "There's a lot going on inside me, and I hate it all. I-I don't even feel like writing. I just feel..." *Defeated.* If anything that word summed up his feelings. He'd rather feel anything else. Something other than numb and stuck. And helpless. So very helpless.

TJ nodded and turned back to his game. "We can get you someone to talk to if you don't want to talk to me."

Freddie dropped his head back on the headboard. Well didn't that just add more guilt to the emotions churning from his gut to his brain. Up and down, round and round, non-stop. TJ's kindness almost had him in tears again. He owed his friend something, because TJ was right, as lead singer of the band, he did have a lot of responsibilities right now. Cancelling tour stops was a huge nightmare no way around it. *What a mess.*

Freddie squirmed, trying to find a comfortable position. Maybe he should get drunk? Like down an entire bottle of some horrid tasting whiskey. "Does the fridge have any of those little bottles of alcohol?"

TJ turned and arched a brow then just shook his head. "No alcohol while on your pain meds."

"Do you think I'm too thin?" Freddie wasn't sure why that question had popped out of his mouth other than his thoughts were all over the place. How had he come to this moment? What *about* him said, *sure, it's okay to hit me?* Maybe he should eat more protein and start a weight-lifting program.

TJ's gaze remained on the game, his fingers pushing the controller's buttons in complicated sequences. "No. I think your body is hot as hell. I'd do you. Or I should say, I've done you, and I'll do you again." He winked then gave Freddie a thorough once over. "Yeah, I'd do you right now if you'd let me. I thought I made that clear?"

Freddie chose to ignore the lust rising between them, as he wasn't in any condition to do anything about it, even though they were alone—and in bed. A big bed. A bed with a comfort top that he'd sink into as TJ sank into him. He blinked and shook his head. *Whoa!* "Whatever. I don't know about all that." He sniffed and twisted a little on his side, facing TJ. "Do you think, I'm...like too gay or something?"

"That's dumb. And that's me dead." TJ sighed then tossed his controller aside. "What does too gay even mean?"

Freddie picked a fluffball off the blanket "I mean, do I seem effeminate or something? Like weak?"

"Are you blaming yourself for that asshole breaking your hand, because don't do that."

Freddie glanced at the TV screen where Kratos was frozen in a fight scene with Hercules. "You ever notice how all the guys on these games are like super-buff with like ladder abs and huge muscles. It's so unrealistic. Guys don't look like that...okay, some do, but in general. I mean, why can't video games have a smart, skinny guy taking down the bad guy?"

"What are you even talking about right now?"

Freddie stared up at the ceiling. "I just want to know, why, and I can't figure it out. People have always picked on me, and you've always been there to stop it. But it's time to protect myself. I need to stop waiting for you and relying on you. I need to fix whatever is wrong with me so I don't get hurt again."

TJ leaned over and tucked Freddie's hair behind his ear. "None of this is your fault."

Dang. TJ smelled so clean, like a pine forest with wild animals scampering about. Like a crisp, cool morning outside of a hidden cabin. He wanted to rest his head on TJ's chest and just breathe in that scent until he fell asleep. But he couldn't hide away anymore. He had to find a modicum of inner strength or he'd never feel safe or brave or worthy. "Some of this *is* my fault, but I *am* a man, you know. I can be strong." He waved a hand at the TV's screen. "My muscles may not have muscles, and I may like my hands all over hard muscles, but I'm still a man. I dealt with all that verbal abuse from my Dad growing up, and now this with Kyle, I feel like I have a sign on my back that says, Kick Me."

"I know you can be strong." TJ took his left hand and squeezed lightly. "I've seen you stand up to your Dad before, and you can do the same with Kyle. And, Daz, it's okay to have others protect you. We want to, okay?"

"Yeah, okay."

TJ shuffled closer and then shot him a sly grin. His hand wandered down Freddie's inner thigh and edged closer to his cock. "But you can show me how much of a man you are, if you'd like."

"Oh my gosh, TJ." He shoved TJ's hand from his thigh. "I'm having a crisis and you're flirting?"

"Yes." On his side, TJ bent his arm at the elbow and rested his chin on his open palm. "You obviously need me to remind you of how beautiful you are."

Freddie shook his head, trying to ignore his now aching cock. "I feel...soft...like what my Dad always says, and I've proven him right. I didn't fight back hard enough. I let Kyle hurt me again."

"Don't do that." TJ trailed a finger down his arm. "Don't let either one of them make you doubt your strength."

"My father's words are a part of me, and that's probably why I let guys hit me."

"*One* guy. You're not taking any blame for this."

"Then neither should you."

TJ sucked in a deep breath, opened his mouth to speak but then closed it. He fiddled with the edge of the white pillowcase for a moment. "I don't agree with that, but moving on, Kyle's been fired. And if you're really wanting to make a change, maybe we can set you up with some self-defense classes."

"I want a gun."

"Freddie." TJ started shaking his head.

"I don't feel safe." Freddie shifted so he was mirroring TJ's stance. "Listen, Kyle said... he said, he would never let me go. He was kneeling over me, breaking my fingers, and he said...he said—"

"Hey...shhh...shhh..." TJ ran his fingers through Freddie's hair. "It's okay."

"How can you look at *me*, look at *my hand*, and say it'll be okay when it isn't?"

"Because in the end, it's *you* that makes everything okay. You've kept me sane. You've kept me believing in our band and myself. *You* are the reason we've made it this far. Nothing has ever meant more to me than you. I don't deserve your friendship, your love, and I've never deserved your devotion. But it's always been you and me ever since that day on the playground, and it'll always be you and me, facing the world together."

"Until when?" Freddie whispered the words, afraid to hope or believe, even when TJ looked so sincere. His body so close.

His lips soft and pink, speaking words he needed to hear. Freddie's cock was already a believer, thick and hard and seeking action versus speeches. Freddie wanted to be on board too, anything to make him forget his messed up life for a few moments.

"Until forever. Apparently your hearing was affected somehow, because I just made another awesome love-speech. I think I need to start writing the lyrics for the band."

"Might as well. I can't write anything with this hand."

"Stop. You can and you will." TJ grabbed Freddie around his middle and drew him closer.

"He destroyed my hand." Freddie let his lower lip jut out, hoping TJ would take the bait and bite. Hard.

"That's yet to be determined."

"I'm broken."

"I'll fix you, because I need that hand wrapped around my dick." TJ kissed him, a soft press of lips against his. "The way you twirl your sticks gets me hard every time."

"Does it?" Freddie lifted his knee until it nudged against TJ's balls, because why not? Why not be daring? Be selfish. They'd been here before as kids. Every move and touch was etched into his memory, and he'd grab on to it again while he could. Add more memories and screw the consequences.

Freddie pressed even harder between TJ's legs, nudging the man's full balls and hard cock.

TJ groaned, pressing his lips to Freddie's again. Tentative at first until Freddie opened for him and sucked on his tongue.

Gasping, TJ pressed him back against the bed and then kissed him harder, slanting his lips over Freddie's at the perfect angle to drive deep.

This kiss turned hot and wet. Became everything Freddie had craved for so long. Perfection with a sweet hint of mint in each tangle and press of TJ's tongue against his. Anticipation and steamy need shot straight to his very eager cock.

TJ eased back, his lips wet and plumped pink. He tugged down the blanket, bent, and licked at the wet spot on Freddie's light blue boxer briefs. Then he used his tongue to trace the outline of Freddie's Animal tattoo. "I still can't believe you got this."

"You're not the only bad boy in this band."

TJ smirked then slid a finger under the boxer briefs elastic band. He pulled it down and locked it under Freddie's balls. "Fuck." He slid a finger along Freddie's hard cock. "Look at that vein. This is the only place you should ever be purple."

"What?" Freddie scoffed. "My dick isn't purple."

"It is a little." TJ glanced up at him and grinned.

"Stop making fun of my dick."

"Fine, I'll just rub it instead."

As TJ stroked up and down his cock, Freddie hissed and dropped his head back. "This isn't a good idea. My minds all messed up, and you're not in a good place either. We shouldn't. Oh, yes...okay, but maybe...that right there..." The words were coming out of his mouth at the same time his hips were arching into TJ's touch.

"Yeah, you just lie back and enjoy." TJ rubbed a thumb over the slick head of Freddie's dick, circling around the rim before bending and licking the leaking tip. "I believe this started because you need to be reminded how fuckable you are."

Freddie rocked into TJ's hand. "Yes, please, remind me."

TJ shot up and kissed him again, all while stroking his cock in a maddening manner.

He wanted hard and fast, this slow and sensual was killing him, yet at the same time exactly what he needed due to his bruised ribs. He moaned into TJ's mouth, not stopping the searing kiss, never stopping. Screw breathing. They could breathe together.

Yet that familiar tingling sensation shot down his spine and maybe even his soul. *Finally.* Finally, he was in TJ's arms, and the love of his life was kissing him and touching his cock perfectly. Reverently. Piecing him back together bit by bit. Each kiss and each touch, a balm to his pain and insecurities. "I'm gonna come, but I don't want to."

TJ tightened his hand along the side of Freddie's face, holding him in place. "Too bad." He squeezed the tip of Freddie's cock, before beginning that gentle slide, up and down again. "Show me. Let me see that beautiful O-face."

Freddie laughed. "Stop."

"No, not stopping. Not ever." TJ's tone turned serious and then he pecked Freddie's lips. "Show me."

Freddie got lost in TJ's gaze. That hooded look along with that tight fist working him was too much. He jerked, his entire body bowing as he shouted out a curse and spurted in TJ's hand.

Their gazes never broke, and that alone was the hottest thing Freddie had ever experienced. Hot and right. His worried mind and tattered heart had given over to the perfection and avoided all thoughts of future pain while reveling in the feel of his pulsing dick.

Biting his bottom lip, he switched his gaze to TJ's jizz-covered hand, which caused a bit more semen to spurt out the tip of over-sensitized cock. "I must've been pent up."

"Something like that, or maybe I'm just a rock star with your dick." TJ licked his fingers. "Mmm...next time I'll choke on that thick cock and swallow everything that comes with it."

Freddie might've groaned a little at those words but then exhaustion hit him hard. And since he could barely keep his eyes open, he didn't want to get into the discussion of whether there would be a next time, and how soon it would be. Instead, he drifted a bit but jerked his eyes open when TJ eased off the bed. "Where are you going?" Because he hadn't got to touch, to kiss all that pine-scented skin.

"The bathroom. I'm hard as fuck."

Freddie blinked, suddenly feeling a little more awake, but unable to move a muscle. "Stand at the door. I want to see."

"Oh, kinky." TJ waggled his eyebrows before sauntering over to the bathroom. Standing in the doorway, he tugged down his zipper and pulled out his dick.

Maintaining eye contact the entire time, TJ jacked his cock until he arched up on his toes and came with a soft cry, creamy spurts hitting the floor.

Freddie's asshole clenched as the scent of sex drifted through the air. His ass needed that hot release, he wanted to feel it dripping out his hole after TJ fucked him. "That was so hot." He wanted to drop to his knees and lick TJ from base to tip. Freddie rubbed his dick, but his left hand just didn't work as well as his right, reminding him he had a whole lot of trouble in his life and one moment of pleasure couldn't erase that truth.

"Problem?" TJ's gaze smoldered as he stroked his glistening and semi-erect cock. He rolled both balls in his hand and hissed.

"Stop...please, stop." Shivering, Freddie closed his eyes, unable to keep watching or he'd bend over the side of the bed and beg to be filled right then. They'd done enough, anything else would further complicate things and his life was already too complicated.

"Oh, Freddie, I can practically hear those wheels of yours spinning. But know this, we won't be stopping now. This is just the beginning. Or should I say, an inevitability, because this was always the end game, whether you believe me or not."

Unable to respond to that shocking statement, Freddie lifted the blanket over his head and hid until he heard the bathroom door shut and the water turn on. He clutched his good hand to his chest, holding TJ's words close. They overlapped and almost silenced Kyle's, which still beat over and over in his mind.

But then Freddie smiled, a grin that surely filled his entire face. *A beginning,* and with those strongly spoken words drifting through his consciousness, he let a tiny bit of hope shine through. A light just as bright, but just as small as one of TJ's little firefly's.

ELEVEN

"FREDDIE, WHY ARE YOUR CHEEKS SO RED?" TJ TILTED HIS HEAD, *gazing over at Freddie.*

"Uh, I was just remembering some things."

"Things?"

"Yeah, stuff we discussed in the kitchen."

"Oh, right. Stuff."

Freddie rolled his eyes. "Sorry, Ms. Burris. Some of our more intimate details are being left out."

She nodded. "Understandable, but...let me tell you, just imagining you two together. Wow! So hot!"

Freddie busted out laughing, hiding his now even redder cheeks behind TJ's back. "Oh my god."

AFTER THEY'D BOTH EXPLODED ALL OVER HIS HAND, TJ HAD taken his time in the bathroom so that Freddie would sleep. Once he'd wasted enough time and jacked off—again, he'd settled into slightly-uncomfortable leather recliner by the bed and answered emails, texts, and also tried responding to all the fans on social media, but their disappointment got to be too much so he signed off and watched his favorite YouTube gaming channels for a bit. His phone continued to ping, but he ignored the messages.

Freddie slept softly. No loud snores for his Dazzler. He'd been agitated about a half hour ago, but TJ had simply whispered in his ear until he'd calmed. His feelings for Freddie had always been big, but had never carried this edge of fear. Fear over Kyle returning. Fear over hurting their long-time friendship. Fear that Freddie's hand wouldn't be the same.

TJ smiled as Freddie stretched and mumbled, "Whatimezit?"

"Hey, you were getting restless, so I figured you'd wake soon." TJ rounded the bed and sat beside Freddie. "It's about seven. I need to go see Emily, but I wanted to wait and see if you would go with me."

"Sure, sure." Freddie ran a hand over his face. "I need to shower." He met TJ's gaze and then blushed.

"Need any help in the shower?"

"Ugh." Freddie plopped back down. "My eyes won't open and my hand is achy. Plus, I think exhaustion from the tour is starting to catch up with me."

"I'll plop a green tea pod in the coffee machine. Get you some caffeine."

"Thanks."

Freddie's response was muffled by his arm draped over his face. TJ chuckled and headed over to the coffee station to start the brewer. "Hey, they only have Earl Grey. That, okay?"

"Sure."

"But you don't like Earl Grey."

"Yeah, this is true."

TJ grabbed the hotel phone and called the front desk, asking if someone could bring them some green tea. He turned around and caught sight of Freddie now propped against the headboard.

"You didn't have to do that. I could've made do."

"Nah, as much as we pay for these rooms, they should brew that shit for us in gold plated mugs."

"S'nice place though."

TJ nodded and shoved his hands in the front pockets of his jeans. He really wanted Freddie to talk about his experience with Kyle. Share his fears. He had to bite his tongue to stop the questions flying through his head. He'd been texting with Bruce and made very clear his conditions on Kyle's dismissal. Bruce said he'd handle everything and keep an eye out for the man, as he'd already been released. The PR department was having a field day coming up with spins and angles and ways to stop Kyle should he go public with anything.

"TJ, are *you* okay?"

"What?" TJ shifted and considered making his own cup of coffee. "Just a lot on my mind."

"I'm sorry, you know."

"I know you are. We'll get through this. It's all good."

"I should probably apologize and basically get back to work tonight."

"I'll get you caught up."

Freddie nodded then yawned. "TJ."

"Yeah."

"I've been thinking."

"Dangerous proposition, right there." He winked and made his way back over to the side of the bed.

"I know." Freddie shrugged and kept his gaze on his hands, which were folded in his lap. "I don't want to hide what happened to me. The truth will get out eventually, and then what? All the men who've been abused will continue to see it as shameful if I lie and make up a story. Plus, sharing what I've been through will help me, I think. I can't pretend it didn't happen. Men abuse other men. It happens."

TJ considered the statement they'd released this morning about why Apollo had cancelled their tour. They'd used Emily's cancer as the reason, but Freddie was right. With all the scrutiny right now, pictures would surface of Freddie's bandaged hand and bruised cheek. "If you come out with your abuse story, you'll have to deal with the media dissecting every facet of your life. They'll twist the truth and hurt you somehow." He covered Freddie's hands with one of his own. "We need to focus on Emily. So can we weather one storm at a time? Please?"

Freddie jutted out his chin and folded both arms across his chest. "The good outweighs the bad. I won't be silent, and I want others to know it's okay to talk about abuse in *any* relationship."

"I'm not saying your story isn't valid or worth being heard. I'm only saying maybe you should deal with everything going on inside you right now first. Talk to someone about everything you feel so if you had to articulate it in an interview, you could. Plus, we need to deal with the band. Our livelihood. And I'm gonna need you for Emily...and...just...I'll need you, ya know?"

"TJ, of course, and as far as our relationship, can we—?"

TJ's phone rang with his Mom's ringtone. "Hold that thought." He hit the answer button. "Hey, Ma. What's up?"

"I don't know what's happening with your band but it must not be good if you're cancelling the tour."

"See that on the news did you?"

"Yeah." She sighed. "I hate to bring this up at what's obviously a bad time, but—"

"What is it?" TJ's stomach churned.

His Mom cleared her throat. "Uh...Emily's too weak to move to hospice."

He met Freddie's gaze and then reached for his hand.

Freddie's eyes went wide and he scooted closer, wrapping an arm around TJ's shoulders.

He held the phone out a little so Freddie could hear too.

"No restaging this time," his Mom continued, voice shaky. "Her body is just done. One drug after another and those cells just find a detour and begin again. Cancer's the gift that keeps on giving and we need...I need to start letting her go. She's fought for so long, for you, and for me, but we can't ask her to do that anymore. It's time, TJ. I'm sorry. I know you thought we could beat this, but we can't. We've had time with her, we've loved her, and that's all we can ever ask. Please don't ask her to give any more." His mom sobbed into the phone. "Please, baby, just let her know it's okay to stop now. She can be at peace for once. God damn it, for once in her life, let her know it's okay not to fight."

TJ sucked in a breath. His mom was the strongest person he knew, next to Emily, and to hear her cry like that rocked him to his core. He slumped down to the floor, breaking free of Freddie's warm embrace. "Shhh...Mom, it's okay. It's okay. I'll do what you say. I won't like it, but I'll give her what she needs. I've always given her that." He took the tissue Freddie handed him and wiped his face. "I'll be there soon. Tell her for me. Tell her, I'll be there until she...I can't say it. Just until, okay?"

"Okay," his mom sputtered through her tears, the words barely a whisper.

Then after a moment, she said, "I have to go."

And she hung up.

TJ swallowed hard, staring at the phone in his hand. She'd ended the call. And for some reason that sealed it. Her words were final now. Done. The red End button mocking him and his family and their fight against this horrific disease. This disease that had strolled into his family, like a sneaky fox that snarled and bit until nothing was left to feed on. Now it was done and would move on to another victim.

Weren't there books on stages of grief? He'd been in the anger stage since they'd received her diagnosis and he'd never left it. Sure he could put on a good front, pretend his heart didn't shatter every time he saw his frail sister, but he'd never forget, never stop loving her, and he'd never leave the stage where he was pissed as hell that this disease had taken someone he loved. *Never.*

The screen saver on his phone was a shot of his family on the cruise they'd taken two years ago. Happier times. Yet always tinged with a bit of fear. "I don't understand any of this. What's Emily ever done to anyone? Why her? She's the sweetest girl in the world, so why take her?"

Freddie knelt beside him, tissues in hand. His eyes were filled with tears and that alone almost broke TJ again.

Then Freddie drew him into his arms. A safe haven. Warm and solid. Giving and never asking for anything in return. TJ breathed deep through his nose and tried to find some semblance of control. He wasn't the one dying but it sure felt like a part of him was slowly fading away into nothing, and only this tight embrace was keeping him from losing himself to some dark place.

"I love you, TJ. You know I do. I *love you.* I love your family. I will do whatever you need." Freddie eased back and cupped TJ's face between his palms. "I'll call Jackson and have him bring the car around. We'll go now. Leave everything behind. We've got to take care of Emily."

TJ sniffed and wiped his nose with the tissue Freddie had handed him. "It's crazy out there. Those story-mongers and photogs are waiting at the front of the hotel, behind the hotel, loitering in the lobby, the restaurant, and coffee shop. Jerks are everywhere just waiting for us to leave so they can blast us with questions. Bruce said he recognized a couple photographers at the bar, too."

Freddie pressed a kiss to his forehead. "Then I'll call him and we'll figure out how to get out of here without having to deal with any of that. That's his job. You said that earlier...something about boat loads of money, right?"

TJ sighed. "Money didn't save her."

Freddie sucked in a breath. "Oh, baby, I know." He held him tight, rocking TJ back and forth before kissing his temple. "Don't worry about any of that right now." Freddie stood and pulled TJ to his feet. "Let me take care of things this time, and we'll go see Emily. *She's* what matters now."

"Freddie...I-I just don't...." TJ shook his head and wrapped both arms around his body. Why was he shaking? His mouth was dry as a desert. And his chest ached. "Freddie, I need to ask this of you. Could I please just go see her first? I need to say...to say..." he swallowed, unable to continue.

"Good-bye. You need to say good-bye." Freddie nodded, wiping away his tears with the wadded tissue in his hand.

TJ closed his eyes. "I don't know if I can."

Freddie squeezed TJ's hand. "I don't know if you can either. I don't know if I can, but...we will, and we'll do it together. I'll give you your moment. Some quiet time with your sister. You both deserve that, but don't for one second think you have to do this alone. I've always been at your side. And you said you want me here now, well don't hurt me again by making that untrue. *You* said relationship, not me. *You*. So, that's what happens in a relationship, you share the pain. Sucks but...we also shared some pleasure earlier." He gave a lopsided grin. "Didn't we?"

"Yeah, we did." TJ inhaled deeply, centering himself. "I won't handle this well. You know this."

"And you know, I'll kick your butt."

TJ shook his head, scoffing a little. "Daz, you just keep on living that dream, 'cause you ain't kicking anyone's butt."

"Well that may be true, but I *can* hire someone to kick your ass." Freddie's eyes narrowed and he stepped right into TJ's space. "Just watch me." He raked his fingers through TJ's hair, tugged on his head, and locked their lips together in a strong kiss. A kiss that said, I will protect and love you.

His Freddie. Precious and beautiful. And everything he'd need to get through the coming days.

Licking his lips as he eased away from the breath-stealing kiss, TJ chucked his drummer under chin. "That was perfect and exactly what I needed." He paused, staring into those sympathy-filled blue eyes. "I'll probably be a dick and say I'm fine, but I won't be."

Freddie smiled and pressed a soft kiss on TJ's lips. "You're always a dick."

TJ held his forehead to Freddie's. "I don't deserve you. But I love you too, Freddie Davis. I love you too."

TWELVE

TJ EXCUSED HIMSELF FROM THE ROOM.

Freddie watched him leave, his heart aching.

Ms. Burris cleared her throat. "I'm very sorry."

Freddie swallowed hard. "Emily was a beautiful girl. I try to remember her that way. Such a fierce little thing." He smiled, but felt the tears start. "Everything was just horrible during that time. Horrible...but RuPaul says, 'It's very easy to look at the world and think, this is all so cruel and so mean. It's important to not become bitter from it.' And so that's what I've tried to do. For a time, everything was cruel and mean, but TJ and I came out stronger in the end. I'm proud of us both and how far we've come. I'm proud that I can sit here and speak about one of the most horrific moments of my life."

"You're a RuPaul fan, huh?"

"Absolutely. Think about all her first steps. I imagine none of that was easy for her, and yet, because of her so many other people feel free to be who they really are. She's the Queen."

"I'll agree with you on that."

Freddie chuckled. "You better, or this interview would be over."

.   .   .

WALKING THROUGH THE HOTEL, FREDDIE FREQUENTLY glanced over his shoulder. Sure that Kyle would pop out of nowhere and beat him down. Moments he'd hoped for with TJ were now coming to fruition, and he hated that his fear tainted everything. The hairs on the back of his neck stood at attention, and his whole body was taut as he followed Bruce into the garage to the waiting car. He had a horrid suspicion that things with Kyle were not quite finished. He scowled at his hand, all wrapped up and a glaring reminder that he was wise to be cautious and aware of his surroundings.

Dressed in a white button down shirt, violet comfort-fit jeans, and his custom-made deep purple loafers, he'd left separately from TJ. His friend was all decked out in one of his many disguises. A brown wig, beefy moustache, white dress shirt, blue tie, khaki pants, and a bit of a padded gut, completed what TJ referred to as his "Milton from *Office Space*" costume. With that get-up and the thick lenses on his face, Apollo's lead singer was actually quite indistinguishable.

Once settled in the backseat, Freddie chatted a bit with Jackson, the band's driver. Trying to distract his mind with the mundane things in life, like the weather and traffic.

"How's Ms. Emily doing, Mr. Davis?"

"Jackson, please stop calling me, Mr. Davis."

"Will do, Mr. Davis."

Freddie chuckled then bit his bottom lip, turning to gaze out the window at all the buildings passing by. "She's at the end. While I don't want her to die, I know it's time. TJ will be a mess. I know you're a religious man, Jackson, so maybe offer up some prayers for his family." He shook his head. Maybe prayer would help, he didn't ever really know, but he had to have faith in something. Family was worth praying over. Heck, he should probably do it more, but his father had kind of ruined religion for him. He believed but not in the way his father did. His father's God was judgmental and unforgiving. Freddie believed that God was love, pure and simple. "Speaking of prayer, I guess I should call my Mom."

"Always a good thing, Mr. Davis." Jackson chuckled then hummed some song to himself as he made his way through traffic.

Freddie sighed. A long sigh, one he frequently found himself doing when thinking of his family. At a stoplight, he thumbed on his phone. "Call Mom."

It rang four times before she answered, "Hello, Freddie."

"How are you?" He forced a cheerful tone into his words.

"We're doing well."

"Since I'm still in town, I thought I'd come by." His stomach, which was already sour due to fear-for-his-life and Emily's condition, churned at the thought of this upcoming visit.

"Oh, well, all right. It's kind of short notice for tonight though." She paused before asking, "How is Emily doing?"

Since he and TJ grew up together, and were in the band together, his mom and TJ's were actually friends of a sort. Even though when he and TJ were still in school, their mom's were not in the same social-bracket. He didn't really want to visit his father, but he did want to see his mom. They were shopping buddies. They'd even done spa days together on the sly. He'd planned to spend some time with her during this tour stop in Chicago but hadn't yet had a chance. Plus, his father would see the results of Kyle's abuse and go on a rant about his "pussy" son for hours. He blinked and focused once again on his Mom's question. "Uh, well, from what I understand, Emily's at the end of her time."

"I'm sorry to hear that. Sheila must be beside herself."

"It's really hard on the *whole* family, yeah." He cleared his throat. "So what day should I come over?" He didn't say 'come home', because his childhood home hadn't deserved that name in years. His place in California was his home now. TJ had just purchased a big house there too, with this amazing ocean view. The designer he'd hired had decorated it all wrong though. Not that TJ spent much time there anyway, since their band was always bouncing from city to city.

Dishes clanging together sounded on the line.

"Are you doing dishes?"

"Yes. The housekeeper couldn't come this week, so I'm doing some general cleanup. I better not break a nail."

Freddie chuckled.

"Well, anyway, when you visit, will you...uh...will you be alone?"

"Yes, Mom. I'll be alone."

"What about Kyle?"

"We've ended things." Freddie glanced ahead as the car slowed. A few reporters were stationed in front of the cancer center, and their heads shot up as Jackson drove under the portico. "It's just me now."

His mom sniffed. "Your father does try."

No. No, his father didn't. But Freddie wouldn't rehash that argument with his mother. Not with his fragile mindset.

"Let's try for dinner tomorrow," his Mom offered. "I'll grab something from the store."

"I don't have to eat so don't change any menus for me. I'll schedule to be there around seven so you won't have to worry about feeding me." Plus his parents went to bed at nine religiously so he'd be in and out in a jiff.

"All right. I'll speak to you later. Keep me up to date about Emily."

After saying goodbye, Freddie stared at his phone for a moment, refusing to become upset about his relationship with his father.

He'd cried over his father's disgust enough. He still had his mother, and TJ's family, and the band. That was all he needed.

This solo trip to the hospital had served a good purpose. His heart ached over losing Emily too, but he needed to be strong for TJ.

He tapped on the divider window.

It lowered but Jackson was on the phone. He was saying a lot of "yes, sir's", so he was likely speaking to Bruce about how to safely transfer Freddie into the building.

Jackson hung up and turned slightly. "Mr. Davis, Bruce says you're to wait until he comes over with one of his men. So, just sit back now. Won't be long."

Freddie glanced out the window as the reporters crowded the car. On the other side of the feeding frenzy, he caught glimpses of people in shorts, t-shirts, and summer dresses. No one was smiling really. Cancer sucked all the happiness right off your face. He needed to find some happiness, wipe the doom and gloom off his own face before he went inside and was surrounded by sadness. Hadn't Emily always told him to appreciate what he had? To be more grateful and kind? He donated a lot of money to cancer research and was sure TJ did the same though they'd never really discussed it.

Catching sight of Bruce barreling out of the building with another big security member at his side freaked Freddie out a little. Here was another muscle-laden guy who could beat him senseless. What if this guy was Kyle's friend? Sweat trickled down Freddie's back and he sucked in a deep breath. No, Bruce wouldn't let anything happen to him. He pressed his shaky hands against his jeans while mentally repeating, "don't be scared" over and over.

When the door opened, he shrieked and placed a hand against his thrumming heart. "Oh, sweet crickets, you startled me."

Bruce leaned into the car. "Let's get you inside, Mr. Davis."

Freddie nodded. "Right. Let's go." And as he stepped out of the car, he forced himself to smile for all the cameras. *Nothing to see here. All is well.*

As Bruce and the security team member corralled him forward, he stiffened for a moment as he was jostled around. He sucked in a long wave of humid air. Sweat instantly formed on his upper lip and brow in the thick heat—just another steamy Chicago afternoon.

Ignoring the shouted questions and the cell phones in his face, Freddie held his head high. He wouldn't be afraid. He could do this.

Hopefully, the photos wouldn't catch the fading-purple bruise still on his cheek. Eyes on Bruce, he almost missed a step at the curb and had to grip the new security guy's shoulder. He quickly jerked his hand back and drew it into a fist at his side. He should've been looking around in case Kyle was lurking by the door.

All these people crushing him were making him sweat even worse. *Gross.* Why hadn't he thought to bring an extra shirt? His fingers were starting to ache, but his pain didn't matter. All these people hurling leading questions at him didn't matter. His worries over Kyle, his father, his mom, and his future as a drummer didn't matter. What mattered was inside those doors. TJ Hardcastle finally needed him again.

———

Skin damp and his shirt sticking to his back, Freddie shivered at the extreme temperature difference from inside to out.

Bruce led him down the hallway to Emily's room. They'd left the new security guy by the elevator. The cancer center smelled of lemons with a not-so-subtle hint of bleach. He'd always had his cleaning people use lavender-scented products, a practice he'd continue now that he'd associate citrus cleaners with death and despair.

Emily had a private room in the back corner of a very quiet floor—a perk mostly likely available due to TJ's money and influence.

Bruce stopped in front of the door and offered a wan smile. "Here you go, kid. And hey"—he gripped Freddie's arm—"don't you worry about Kyle. I took care of it."

"Okay." Freddie nodded. He offered Bruce a reassuring smile he didn't really feel before facing the door to Emily's room again. After taking a deep breath, he knocked once and then entered the room.

TJ was sprawled out in a metal chair with both elbows on the armrests and his head bent over his phone.

Freddie shook his head. How did he not have a crick in his neck?

Next to TJ sat his Mom, Sheila, and his younger sister, Megan. The teen glanced up from her hardbound book titled, *The Immortal Life of Henrietta Lacks*. Big book for such a tiny, brunette. Her nails were painted a teal color, and her hair was up in a messy ponytail-bun thing. Her smile didn't quite reach her eyes, which made the sadness and hopelessness drifting through the room all the more pervasive. Almost cloying in its grip. Like a real entity that forced you to realize its existence and make you feel the pain of death, soon, so very soon.

Some cooking show played on the flat screen mounted on the wall in the corner.

Emily rested on the hospital bed, coughing into her hand that held a small battery-operated fan, apparently it helped with the breathlessness.

He winced when the cough didn't end and racked her tiny body. Her breast cancer cells had danced their way into her lungs.

And even after all the treatments and medicines they'd stayed and partied her life away.

Light purple bruises colored the skin beneath her red-rimmed eyes and her skin seemed paper-thin. A memory of her on the cheer squad in high school shot through his mind, and he fought not to compare the two images.

With her other hand resting at her side, she lifted it a little in a slight wave and then took a deep breath before smiling at him.

That radiant smile when things were so bleak broke his heart. An event that would likely occur over and over as this process continued. He dug deep and brought forth a smile before shuffling over to her side. For some reason, he felt as if he should be very quiet which made no sense, and yet, once beside the bed, he still whispered, "I've missed you."

With that smile and her bright brown eyes, he caught another glimpse of the girl he remembered from so long ago, back when she was healthy and whole. He'd make sure to get pictures of her framed and put in his home. He had plenty, and he wanted to remember her that way. She'd want that, too. He'd keep her in the one place that mattered since he couldn't have her anywhere else.

"'Member what we talked about?"

He clenched his jaw as her words came out on puffs of air as if she fought to release each syllable from her mouth. He nodded because he couldn't speak. A few years ago, she'd made him promise that when she died, he'd take care of TJ. He'd hemmed and hawed, saying she'd be there to do so, and when she'd gotten angry, and very blunt about her condition, he'd made the promise. But faced with the reality of fulfilling that promise, he was suddenly furious over the unfairness of it all. Not that he had to take care of TJ, but that he had to say goodbye to this beautiful woman. That even in her current pain, her thoughts were of others and not herself.

Emily reached over and tapped his hand, feather light, like a little bird prancing on his wrist. "My pretty Freddie." Nodding, she coughed again before turning away and closing her eyes.

"Hey, there." Sheila stood and wrapped Freddie in her arms for a long moment before finally pulling away and meeting his gaze. "Oh honey, you look tired. Come sit." She glanced at her daughter and the pain in her eyes was so clear that Freddie wanted nothing more than to whisk them all away to someplace safe and disease free.

TJ grabbed Freddie's arm and tugged him toward the door. He spoke over his shoulder while he dragged Freddie from the room. "We need a minute."

Freddie heard, Megan hollering, "He just got here."

"We'll be back." TJ hadn't stopped their forward motion. He'd dumped the majority of his costume, but still wore the white button down shirt and khaki pants, which were bunched together at his waist and held up with a brown belt.

Out in the hall, TJ passed Bruce with a grunt and then skidded to a stop in front of the Family bathroom. He shoved Freddie inside and then locked the door.

Unclear what was happening, Freddie turned to face him. "TJ, what are you—"

"Shut up." TJ kissed him, pressing him against the door.

Freddie eagerly kissed him back, reveling in TJ's coffee-with-a-hint-of-chocolate taste.

TJ pulled back, gasping for breath before pressing his forehead against Freddie's. "I need you." He yanked on his belt.

"Whoa." Freddie gripped TJ's hand. "What are you doing?"

TJ arched a brow. "I'm trying to free my dick."

"Um...TJ, don't you think this isn't maybe such a good time? And not only that, it smells like rotted diapers in here."

"Fred." TJ ran a hand through his hair. "I can't do this. I can't...

Emily...she... and I just want to feel something else. I want to drown in you."

Oh that sounded so good, and inviting, and so very hot that Freddie felt his insides melt just a little more. "Hey, let's think about this, please." Freddie wrapped TJ in his arms. "Listen, it's okay. I've got you." He ran a hand up and down TJ's back. "We're not having sex in this bathroom. We're going back into that room and sitting with your sister. I won't let you make this about you and your pain. So stop."

"That's a shitty thing to say, Daz."

"You can be kinda selfish. Everyone knows this. You've proven it time and again, but I won't let you today. I'll hold you together, but not in this bathroom and not in this way. I'm sorry, but I just don't think sex is the answer." He eased back and squeezed TJ's shoulder. "Okay?"

"No, it's not okay. Sex is always the answer, and I don't like you very much right now."

"I don't really care, and you love me. Already said it earlier so no takebacks." He waved a hand toward the overflowing trashcan. "We're done in here, and we're going back to your sister's room." He stepped out into the hallway and held the door open for TJ. "After you."

TJ narrowed his eyes. "Fine. Whatever."

"I forgot you're still twelve."

"Shut up."

Freddie chuckled, but inside he was questioning his choice. Perhaps he should've let TJ find comfort in sex, but honestly, baby poo stench was not conducive to maintaining an erection.

On the way back to the room, his phone rang with the *Rocky* theme ringtone. He froze in place. Kim had given him his phone back at the hospital but he hadn't really had time to catch up on any messages. And now, terror was calling from the front pocket of his jeans.

TJ came up beside him and narrowed his eyes. "What's wrong?"

He braced a hand against the wall, and his heart started beating like mad. "N-nothing. It's n-no one."

His phone went off again. Same ringtone. Same icy fear racing down his spine.

"Why won't you answer that?" Head tilted to the side, TJ flicked a finger toward the phone.

"No, I don't...it's okay." Freddie avoided TJ's gaze and took a deep breath.

"Is Kyle calling you?"

Freddie's phone chimed, indicating a voicemail before it rang again.

"Why haven't you blocked his number?" TJ reached for him, but Freddie stepped back and slapped his hand away.

"I've been a little busy. I don't spend all my time on my phone like you do."

"Nah, nah, don't be spinning this off onto me. Give me your phone. We're listening to that message, right the hell now. Then we're forwarding it to Bruce."

"I don't want to listen to it."

"Oh really, who just denied me in the bathroom because he said I couldn't avoid things?" TJ reached into his pocket and pulled out Freddie's phone. "Passcode, now."

Freddie sighed but gave him the code.

TJ pressed the voicemail button, and Kyle's hard tone came across very clearly in the quiet hall.

"Enough is enough, Freddie. You made me talk to that quack and then just left me. You said we could work things out then like a pussy

you ran. Then you get me fired? Your ass is mine, literally. I'll show you who owns you. Answer your phone. You'll be sorry if you don't."

Another message signal chimed, so TJ hit Play.

"Quit being a baby. Couples fight. It's natural. Just talk to me, Freddie. You said you'd try. I won't let you leave me."

Those last words sent chills down Freddie's spine. How far was Kyle willing to go? How desperate was he? "Please, just delete them. We don't have time for that nonsense." Freddie went for blasé and hoped TJ didn't notice his shaky hands.

"How many messages has he left like this?"

Freddie shrugged and looked down the hall before facing him again. "We should get back to your sister."

"Oh, no. Don't avoid the question." TJ stormed down the hall and stopped in front of Bruce.

Freddie could only follow.

TJ held the phone out to Bruce. "Kyle is leaving nasty, threatening messages on Freddie's phone. Take this and buy him another."

Freddie blinked. "What? I need my phone."

Bruce glanced at the phone then him. "We'll take care of this and get you another. We should've had you block his number before now. I'm sorry you had to deal with him again."

"Bruce, I'm not a child. I can block him myself."

"Then why didn't you?" TJ stood with both hands on his hips.

"I've been a bit distracted. Sorry. I'll do it now." He held out his left hand. "Bruce, my phone, please."

"Mr. Davis, I need to forward this to the police and your lawyers."

"Yes, Freddie, he needs to handle this so you're going to let him."

"TJ. Bruce. I'll hand over the phone, but please, let me be the one to block his number. It's a small step, but one I have to take myself."

Bruce nodded and handed over his phone. Then they both hovered as he blocked Kyle's number.

"There." He gave a stiff nod. "That felt good and you may now have my phone to do with as you please, but I'll need a replacement ASAP. All right?"

"Yes. I'll be right back." Bruce took his phone and headed down the hallway toward the elevators.

When Freddie turned back to TJ, he caught the man staring at him. "What?"

"I'm proud of you."

Freddie felt his cheeks heat. "Thank you." He jerked his chin toward Emily's door. "Let's focus on her. Don't worry about me. I'll be okay."

"We'll have to deal with Kyle again at some point, you know? He's obviously not giving up on you. Guy is mental." TJ ran a hand over his face before stretching his arms over his head.

Freddie took a moment to admire TJ's sleek lines. "Yeah, he is but I don't want to think abut him right now or talk about him. Let's go back inside." He placed a hand on TJ's back and led him into the room.

Sitting beside TJ, he spent the next couple hours getting caught up on Megan and Sheila's lives and tried to shake the absolute panic still firing through his blood. Kyle continued to taunt him. To torment him. And though he'd try to convince TJ—and himself otherwise, he was frightened of what Kyle might do next. His imagination had him locked in some cold basement, getting sprayed with a hose. He'd pray that Bruce and his team would keep anything from interfering with his time saying goodbye to Emily. And though they all avoided discussing that very real truth, that's why they were here—to say goodbye.

THIRTEEN

TJ SAUNTERED BACK INTO THE ROOM, A SHEEPISH LOOK ON HIS face.

Knowing they might need a moment to talk, Freddie turned to the reporter. "Ms. Burris, would you like some lunch? I'm sorry we've kept you so long, but now that I'm ready to tell the story, I feel I must to do it justice by being very transparent."

TJ grabbed Freddie's drumsticks off the coffee table and twirled them in his hand. "I can order Thai."

"Chef Will prepared both lunch and dinner."

"Yeah, but I want Thai."

Freddie sighed and twisted his neck side to side. "Then get Thai."

TJ grinned, "Nah, you're right. I'll just grab Will's stuff."

"I will kill you one of these days. You drive me absolutely mental."

"Ms. Burris, did you hear that? Here he is talking about non-violence, and yet he threatens to murder me daily."

Ms. Burris chuckled. "I think you're just fine."

"Yes." TJ winked "I am."

Freddie groaned. "That's gross. Come on, let's chat in the kitchen for a moment."

TJ nodded before leading the way. "Where are you in the story now?"

"I gave her a condensed version of going to the cancer center and Kyle's text messages."

TJ grunted. "The next part sucks."

Freddie wrapped his arms around TJ from behind. "I can go on alone, you know."

"Nah, I'll stick this out." TJ turned his head and kissed him. "Now, fix me some lunch."

Freddie bit his earlobe and whispered, "I thought I fed you earlier."

TJ turned and fully faced him. "Damn, quit talking naughty when we have strangers in the house."

Freddie grinned and swatted TJ's ass. "I wasn't naughty until you so...all your fault."

TUGGING THE COKE BOTTLE FROM THE BOTTOM OF THE vending machine, Freddie handed it to TJ. "Sugar in liquid form. Yum."

TJ nodded, unscrewing the lid and taking a long sip. The sugar hit his tongue and he savored the rush. He had so much to do. So many calls to return, texts, and emails, but right now, he just wanted to talk to Freddie. Needed to expel everything. Needed Freddie to write him a song so he could sing the words and free his mind from this constant swirl of thoughts. Anything to take the weight off his chest. "Freddie."

"Yes, TJ."

"I hate cancer."

"I know."

"I hate hospitals. Everything is just so...dire." He swirled the liquid around in the bottle, keeping his gaze on the bubbling brown liquid. "But what I hate most is that my sister is dying, and I can't do a thing to stop it. I can't breathe for her. I can't take her pain away. The whole thing just pisses me off."

Freddie clapped a hand against his shoulder. "Me, too."

TJ put his hand over Freddie's and squeezed. "Let's go back."

He stopped at the door but couldn't go inside. He slid down the wall and pulled Freddie beside him onto the cool floor.

TJ sighed and set the bottle on the ground. "I worked for her future, ya know? I had everything planned out, money put away, and hopes for her. So much hope. I sweat and scream on that stage so my family can have a better life, but that hard work didn't matter. Nothing I do changes anything."

"That's not true." Freddie tipped up his chin. "Emily is so proud of you, and she loves you. More than anything."

TJ snorted out a half-laugh. "And where does that get her? She's twenty-two years old and she's essentially dead. How does her love for me, or mine for her, make any difference?"

"Love makes all the difference. And you *did* make her life better. You made her care better. You eased your mother's burden. Just imagine if she had to borrow money from my parents again." Freddie shook all over. "Borrow from my Dad."

"Yeah, that sucked."

"TJ, I know seeing Emily this way...hurts, and I know nothing makes sense." Freddie rested his head back against the wall. "When this is over, I'll write her a song, and maybe you'll sing it."

"I was just thinking that." TJ shook his head. "You know me."

"Yeah?"

"Yeah."

"Writing the song will hurt. Singing it will hurt even more."

Freddie squeezed TJ's knee. "But Emily wants you to live. She always has. I'll always remember that time the three of us were in the car together and Apollo's first single came on. She sang along with you. And I'd never heard anything more beautiful."

"I remember." TJ swallowed hard. "She can sing, right?"

"She can."

"I don't think I can let her go. Not today. Maybe never."

Freddie kissed the side of his head before resting his cheek against TJ's shoulder. And that was...nice. Comforting. He squirmed while considering his selfish request for sex earlier, because Freddie was right—this softer moment was more of what he truly needed. He was so exhausted from the tour, from worry over everything, and yet, he couldn't shut his brain down long enough to sleep. Freddie's breathing had evened out, so he sat quietly for a moment, thinking that maybe he could shut his eyes too.

Just as his heavy lids closed, he jerked awake when Freddie screamed.

"Whoa, Freddie, hey, hey, it's okay. You're safe."

Freddie blinked over and over. "Where? What happened?"

"You must've had a bad dream."

"Was I asleep long?"

"No."

"Oh." Freddie frowned. "Well, that isn't good news."

"I'm sorry, Daz. You shouldn't have nightmares. I should've done more."

Freddie pressed a finger against TJ's lips. "Stop. You're not to blame in any of this."

"That doesn't mean I'm not sorry for what happened to you." TJ brought Freddie's hand to his lap and played with his fingers. "For a long time now, I've taken you, the band, and my family for granted, but I-I won't do that anymore."

"Let's not talk about that now."

He supposed he deserved Freddie's continued reticence. His drummer had casually sidestepped each comment about building their relationship into something more. While fair, Freddie's doubt still stung.

TJ turned and studied the man beside him. God he was stunning. His long lashes, covering those crystal blue eyes. Those strong drummer's arms. His angular jaw, and his nose the perfect shape for his face. "I bet you still suck dick like a champ."

"What?" Freddie gasped. "What the heck, TJ? We're out here having a nice moment. I'm worried as hell about you, and you're sitting there thinking about...well...*that*."

TJ just grunted.

Freddie arched a brow, in a challenging way. "I do suck dick like a champ. Best you'll ever have, and yeah, I know you have a lot to compare me too, but I don't care." He sing-songed. "I'm the best ever. No contest."

"I carry no shame over my active sex life. No shame at all." He shrugged. "Although, I must say, your jealous face is kinda cute."

"I hate you."

"No you don't."

"Sometimes, TJ. Sometimes. Especially when I think about—"

"Don't." TJ cupped Freddie's sweet face in his palm before lightly kissing his lips, nibbling on the bottom one. "I'll earn your trust again. I want this. I want you."

Freddie licked his bottom lip. "Okay, Hardcastle. We'll see what we see."

TJ nodded and huffed out a long sigh. "I'll get you to believe me. Somehow. Some way."

Freddie met his gaze for a moment and then nodded. "Sure. We'll discuss this again when we've both slept for a week."

He was quiet for a moment, then he shifted a little, ready to get up and head back into his sister's room. "My ass is numb from sitting on this floor."

Freddie rolled his eyes. "TJ."

"Yeah?"

"I just want to say...that I'm sorry, too. You wish you could take away everyone's pain, but I feel the same way about you. I'm sorry you have to go through this. I know the timing of everything is off, and we got a lot weighing on us now with the tour and just...you know, life, but whatever happens from this moment on...know that I love you and...I don't know how to make you feel not sad, because there isn't anything I can say or do really...b-but I'll be here, okay? Just don't forget that." He dropped his gaze. "Don't forget me."

TJ's chest ached at Freddie's tone. His friend had always been a little insecure. Unsure and a bit feeble, but he had the biggest heart that just gave and gave and asked for nothing in return. Yet, Freddie had found the strength to ask now, and TJ couldn't deny him. "I will never forget you, Daz." He drew Freddie into his arms and pressed a kiss to the top of his head. "We'll get there. You'll see."

Freddie nodded, his soft hair tickling as it moved back and forth on TJ's neck. "Let's see how Emily's doing."

"Yeah, we should go back in." TJ let Freddie pull him to his feet. He brushed off the back of his pants and glanced down the hall.

A male nurse stood, holding his phone at a weird angle by his side.

TJ stiffened then fury shot through his blood.

How dare he!

How long had he been filming them? He'd likely captured some high-dollar images of their private moment.

TJ should know better, nothing in his life was private. Furious, he stalked down the hall. "Hey! What are you doing?"

Freddie stepped alongside him. "What's wrong?"

The "nurse" tucked away his phone in his front pocket. "I'm standing in a public hallway."

"This is a private floor. How did you get up here?" TJ stepped into the man's space, and caught a glimpse of Bruce's security guy coming over from the elevators. "What the hell do we pay you for? I can spot these freaks a mile away, so why can't you?"

"Is this man bothering you?" The security guard stopped at his side.

"Do you need your hearing checked along with your eyes? Dude, he's taking photos with his phone. What the hell, man? Do your job!"

"TJ."

"No." He brushed off Freddie's grip on his arm and rounded on the fake-nurse. "You think you got a story with those photos, well you know nothing. Get the hell out of here."

Freddie shoved TJ out of the way and jabbed a finger in the photogs face. "Listen here, you parasite. You can say whatever you want about me and TJ, but you better leave his family out of this."

The man wiped a hand across his balding head. "So there is a you and TJ then?"

"Are you serious, right now?" Freddie surged forward.

"Whoa." The security guy stepped in between them. "I've got this."

"You better." Freddie narrowed his eyes. "Get this guy out of here. TJ's right, do your job. These...*people*, they are sneaky and tricky and you better be on your toes because they stop at nothing to get you. How can we trust you when you let this guy slip past? What kind of security are you? Who else has slipped past your defenses? Who else—"

"Hey." TJ gripped a practically feral Freddie by the shoulders. "Hey, look at me. It's all right."

"No, it isn't. Kyle could be here, TJ." His eyes were wide, and he eased away until his back hit the wall. His gaze skipped from the elevator to the hallway. "Kyle could be here."

"No, no, he isn't. He won't."

"You can't know that. This guy got by." Freddie flicked a hand at the fake male nurse.

TJ sucked in a breath. They couldn't talk about this here. Not out in the open. And this guy was hanging on every word. "Freddie, come on. Let's calm down. We'll let this new security person... what's your name?" He glanced at Mr. Italian Stallion in the slick black suit.

"Michael Antonacci."

"Listen, Antonacci, get this creep out of here. Have him arrested for trespassing or whatever and then get me Bruce, all right? Don't let anyone else near us right now, because I'm wanting to hit something real bad, but it'll upset my family, you hear me?" He turned and faced the bald man with the camera full of photos. "And you." He poked the photographer in the chest. "You go ahead and publish those photos of Fred and me. I don't care. You can even add that we're together now. Tell everyone I'm off the market for good. I don't give a shit."

Freddie made an odd sound in his throat, opened his mouth, but nothing came out.

"That's right, Fred. You and me in black and white, maybe then you'll believe." He nodded then whirled on his heel and stomped back to his sister's room.

FOURTEEN

"THAT'S TOO BAD YOU HAD YOUR PRIVACY INVADED." MS. BURRIS *bit daintily into a tortilla chip.*

TJ was glad his mouth was stuffed with taco dip because that stopped him from pointing out her entire purpose for being here today was to invade their privacy.

Freddie sipped from his white wine. He hadn't eaten much, which bothered TJ a little, yet he'd always said he didn't like to eat in front of others. Which made sense, because since they'd announced they were together, they'd been on display—a lot.

TJ had done what he could to protect his drummer's need for privacy. Dropped his social media presence and focused more on loving Freddie and spending time with his Mom and sister. Nothing else mattered. He'd promised to remain at Freddie's side, and so that's what he'd done. "Hey, Daz, you sure you don't want some the chicken?"

Freddie shook his head, "No, I want to get through the next part."

TJ started putting their lunch items away, knowing the worst was yet to come, but knowing they'd get through it. Together.

. . .

FREDDIE TRIED TO SLEEP. HE TOSSED AND TURNED, TRYING TO pull the trigger on what felt like a monumental decision. They were all camped in Emily's room. He and TJ in chairs, and Sheila and Megan on cots. "TJ," he whispered as he shook the man's shoulder. "Hey, wake up."

"What?" TJ's head lolled against the back of the chair but he didn't open his eyes. "Timezzit?"

"What you said to that photographer...was it...was it true?"

"What? Yeah, I already told you that."

"Oh. Well, I want to go to the bathroom then."

TJ groaned. "Go then. Why are you waking me up to tell me that?"

"No, I mean, I want to find a bathroom that doesn't smell like baby poo and give you what you asked for earlier."

TJ opened his eyes. "What I asked for earlier?"

"I made a decision."

"Right now?"

"Yes, right now."

"But you said bathroom sex was selfish."

"It is, but everyone's asleep now."

"But Emily could wake up."

"We'll be quick."

TJ rubbed his eyes. "Okay."

"Wow, your enthusiasm is more than I can handle." Freddie rolled his eyes.

"I'll give you more than you can handle for waking me out of a deep sleep." TJ shot to his feet and held out his hand. "Let's go."

Freddie stood and took TJ's hand and that was it. Done deal. Sealed. TJ could break his heart again, and likely would, but he'd resolved to take a chance. To jump off the cliff and hope for a soft landing. And he wanted to leap right now. TJ making that public declaration earlier had melted the final doubt from his heart. Plus, he wanted to make a decision for himself, not be pushed around or bullied.

They both needed this moment. He'd show TJ that he wasn't always shy, that he could be naughty when he wanted...and oh, how he wanted.

In the hallway, he pressed against TJ's back.

The security guy, Antonacci stepped in front them and arched a brow. "Can I help you?"

"Yes, you can." TJ took Freddie's hand. "I'm giving you a second chance to do your job right. Here's what's happening. Freddie and I are having a private moment in that bathroom. Keep that to yourself, warn us if anything is going down out here, and knock if something happens in my sister's room, all right?"

The man simply nodded, and then folded both hands together at his waist.

Freddie buried his burning face in the back of TJ's neck. "Oh, my God. We have no privacy in our lives."

TJ tugged him along then shoved him in the family bathroom, shut the door, and locked it. "Smells better."

"Yeah, it does," Freddie agreed then he wrapped his hand around the front of TJ's neck and pushed. "Stand with your back against the door."

TJ smiled a wicked smile. "All right."

Freddie ran his hand along TJ's jaw and then took his mouth in a savage kiss. Over and over, he slanted his mouth, taking and taking, making the moment even more raw than it was. Hot and slick, and meshing and on an edge they'd soon both tumble over.

Raking in a deep breath, he eased back and met TJ's hooded gaze. "Put your hand on my head and press me down."

Eyes flickering with surprise, TJ arched a brow and then kissed him hard before he set his hand to the top of Freddie's head and pressed him down.

On his knees, Freddie licked his lips. "Tug down your zipper."

TJ hissed as he slowly followed Freddie's order.

Freddie wanted them naked. Wanted bare skin. Wanted a bed. Wanted the slide of TJ's hard dick in his ass. He glanced up at TJ from under his lids. His skin was on fire. His senses overwhelmed.

"Is your mouth nice and wet?" TJ panted out the words, gazing down at Freddie.

"Slide between my lips and find out." Freddie tipped up his chin and opened his mouth.

"Oh, that's a pretty sight." TJ gripped a hunk of Freddie's hair. "Gonna fuck that mouth. Gonna stretch your lips and your throat. You ready?"

"Yes." Freddie nodded. "Take out that thick cock."

TJ worked his dick free and then stroked it a couple times. "Huh." His brow furrowed as he glanced down at his hand.

"What?"

"My dick. I think it's broken." He tugged on it a few more times. "Damn it!"

"What's wrong?" Freddie glanced at TJ's dick, which remained semi-soft in his fist. "Oh. Should I try...to...um...do something?"

"No." TJ cursed then leaned back against the wall. His flaccid cock hanging over the top of this dark blue boxer briefs. "This can't be happening."

Fighting back disappointment, Freddie slowly rose to his feet. "I thought you wanted this."

TJ barked out a laugh. "I do. More than anything, but..." He raked a hand through his hair. "I guess I'm just broken." Shaking his head, he stuffed his dick back in his pants. "Freddie, please know it's not you. I wanted to bend you over that sink and pound that sweet ass until I felt something other than this ache in my chest."

He ran a hand over his breastbone. "But...I'm exhausted, and apparently, my dick is exhausted. And I guess..." He breathed in deep. "I think...I'm sad. My sister is dying. You're hurt, and I'm just...I'm sad."

Freddie's heart crumbled into pieces over TJ's softly whispered words. Stepping forward, he wrapped TJ in his arms. "I'm so sorry. I shouldn't have made you do this. I should've let you sleep."

TJ squeezed him tight. "I *do* want you, Daz. So much, but my body won't cooperate right now. I'm sorry."

"Don't be sorry." Freddie ran his hands up and down TJ's back. "Just let me hold you then we'll go back to the room and try to sleep again."

"I think I'm going to cry." TJ croaked as he sucked in a deep breath. "Can you hold me tight? Just hold me together while I break? I can't hold it in anymore, Fred. Everything hurts."

"Oh TJ, of course." Freddie kissed TJ's cheek, running his hands along the back of TJ's head, and pressing his face against his shoulder.

TJ sobbed then. His entire body shaking as he released everything he fought so hard to contain.

Freddie held back his own tears, because this wasn't his moment. This was TJ's.

While moving his hands in circles up and down TJ's back, Freddie whispered soothing words in his ear. This man in his arms was always so strong, so tough, but no one could go through what they had these past few days and not need to lean on a friend. He'd not believed his love for TJ could grow any deeper, but this glimpse into his friend's troubled heart added more layers to his already overwhelming feelings.

After a few more minutes, TJ finally settled, resting his forehead on Freddie's shoulder. "Oh man, I really needed that. Give me a second."

He turned, flipped on the faucet, and then splashed his face with water a few times.

Freddie ripped off some paper towels and handed them over. "Here, dry your face."

TJ patted his rosy cheeks then took a deep breath and slowly let it out. Then he cupped Freddie's face between his hands. "Thank you."

"You're very welcome." Freddie leaned forward and softly kissed him.

Easing back, TJ met his gaze. "What would I do without my Dazzler?"

"I don't think you'll ever have to worry about that."

"I have though, and I do. I will not to mess this up. You see the real me, Fred. You always have. And I know what you see isn't always pretty, but it *is* real, right?"

"Yeah." Freddie grinned then kissed him again. "You can barely keep your eyes open. Let's get you back to that seriously uncomfortable chair." He turned to go, but TJ didn't release him.

"Freddie."

"Yes."

"We will finish this when my entire focus can be on you and only you. And when my dick stops being a dick and decides to work again."

"That look in your eye holds lots of promises, Hardcastle. Let's hope you can deliver."

"I will. You'll see."

"All right." Freddie huffed out a breath. "Now, let me go so I can wash my hands."

TJ sighed but let him go.

At the sink, he met TJ's gaze in the mirror. "It's okay to cry, you know. I cry all the time. Nothing wrong with it."

TJ shrugged and then hip-bumped him away from the sink.

Freddie squawked. "Hey. That's rude."

TJ cleaned his own hands and then ripped a paper towel from the holder. "So this is us now, right?"

"Am I or am I not in a disgusting bathroom with you right now with your snot all over my shoulder?"

"Oh, Fred, you'll come to enjoy all my fluids."

"Is that right?" Freddie rolled his eyes. "Yes, this is us, but don't think this means I'll be starring in any of your ridiculous social media videos. We are not a movie of the week or whatever."

"You love those movies."

Freddie fought back a grin, because yeah, he did, even though they were so cheesy he needed crackers. "TJ."

"Yeah."

"I think we need some music."

TJ tilted his head to the side. "Um...okay."

"No, I mean, I think Emily might like to hear us play something. When Drake and Kim came by, we weren't acting like *us*. And we should still *be* us. We should give her music."

TJ blinked then dropped his gaze. "Oh."

"What...do you think that's a bad idea?"

"No," he said with a soft voice. "I just think you're pretty fucking amazing. And that you always know the right thing to do for my family and for me." He pressed a fist against his chest. "You say things like that and you don't think anything of it, but every time, you hit me right here." He pounded a fist against his heart. "We'll give her music, Fred. And when we're done here, you and me, the band, we'll keep giving her music, because that's what we do."

"She'll hear it." Freddie offered a weak grin, fighting back tears. "She'll always hear it, no matter where we go or what we are to each other. She'll hear it."

TJ stepped forward and pressed his forehead against Freddie's.

"Don't ever stop speaking from your heart, because I'll hear you. I always have."

Freddie closed his eyes. "TJ."

"Yes."

"You're not going to start talking about lightning bugs again, are you?"

TJ laughed and shoved him away. "That was romantic as hell."

"Romance in a Family bathroom full of baby poop? Nah, I think you can do better."

"That right?" TJ kissed him softly then tickled his sides.

"Ahhh, my ribs are still sore, jerk! Plus, you're pressing me against unsanitary surfaces."

"You didn't seem to care earlier."

He chuckled then caught TJ's shiny, brown gaze. "It's good to see a real smile on your face."

"Jesus, Fred, you're hitting me with those words again."

Freddie pressed his palm against TJ's beating heart. "I want to protect this."

"You do." TJ smiled and locked their fingers together. "So, what song should we sing, you think?"

Freddie grinned and led him back to Emily's room. Music had always been their respite and this time was no different. They'd roll with the rhythm they'd always found together, and now that they were in synch once again, Freddie had no doubt they'd give Emily their best work yet.

FIFTEEN

"WELL THAT WASN'T EASY. ARE YOU SURE YOU WANT TO STAY *for rest?"* Freddie's eyes reflected his worry.

TJ tapped his lover's nose with an index finger. "No, I don't really, but I might as well because everyone knows what happened next anyway."

"Cost of fame, right?" Ms. Burris piped up.

TJ glanced at her. He'd kind of forgotten she was even in the room after listening to Freddie retell their story. Luckily, he'd again left out a lot of the "sexy stuff" because recalling that moment of weakness in both his body and spirit was not pleasant. Crying instead of fucking should never be a thing, but it had been. Yet Freddie had been his rock like always. He shook off those thoughts. "To a certain extent, yes, people following my life is the cost of fame. Although, I don't believe my family should ever have to pay the price." He knew his tone held an edge but he hated when news reports included his family. Taking a deep breath, he turned to Freddie. "I can talk about her now. I don't like it, but I can."

Freddie gave him a soft smile. "I know you can."

"I really like it when you smile, Daz."

"Flirting because you don't like the subject isn't going to work. We need to get through this." Freddie took his hand. "Do you want me to tell this part?"

"No. I can."

I N   THE   END ,   E MILY   HAD   TAKEN   THREE   DEEP   BREATHS ,   EYES closed with her fragile hand wrapped around his.

And then her hand went slack.

But TJ couldn't let go.

How could he ever release the girl who'd fallen asleep on his lap after singing all the words to *Beauty and the Beast?* Or the woman so proud of her acceptance into Northwestern? Or the free spirit who sang along with the radio during short trips for ice cream cones?

He'd promised her more. Even declared everything would be fine. And hadn't he given every part of himself so that those words could become true?

Freddie wrapped an arm around his shoulder and sang Vince Gill's "Go Rest High On That Mountain."

TJ sucked in a breath, hating Freddie a little for singing that song. For letting her go.

His mom joined in with Freddie's angelic voice.

And when they finished the song together, TJ's heart cracked in two.

Megan sobs against his mom's shoulder became the only sound in the room other than the rushing in his ears.

Emily's hand was so cold now. "Is...is there a b-blanket in here somewhere? It's cold. Is it cold? I can't tell." His body was shaking and his shirt was sticking to his sweaty back. His stomach churned, and he should probably go lie down somewhere before he passed out. He tried to swallow but his mouth was dry. "I think I need some water or something."

"Theodore James, look at me."

He startled upon hearing his real name and locked his gaze on his Mom's. "What'd I do?"

"Nothing. You're fine." Her lips lifted in a sad smile. "But you need to let her go, baby. She's at peace now."

"Peace." He nodded and stepped back, wiping a hand over his wet face. Was she at peace though? Where had she gone? All he knew was that she wasn't *here* anymore, and he hadn't been able to stop it.

Freddie dropped his arm from around TJ's shoulder and clutched his bicep. "Hey, it's okay. Just breathe."

"I can breathe."

Freddie's brow furrowed. "Yes, you can."

"But...but...sh-she isn't though. So how can I?"

Freddie tried to draw him closer, but he stepped away toward the door.

Just inside the doorway, he braced a hand against the wall. This was it. Once he left this room, he'd have to accept that the struggle was over. One foot across that threshold meant his sister was really gone. His heart thrummed like crazy, and he dropped to his knees. "I can't do this."

Freddie crouched down in front of him and cupped his face between his hands. His eyes were red rimmed and a single tear hung on the edge of his jaw, just waiting to fall.

"Hey, you've gone gray on me. Why don't you come out to the sitting area and we'll have something to drink, okay?"

"But when I leave it's all over, Fred."

"What's over?"

"Everything and it's not fair."

Freddie lifted TJ's chin, holding his gaze. "Don't break on me now. Your Mom and your sister still need you. *I* need you. Come on. Stand up and we'll discuss the next steps."

"What? What steps? That's what I'm saying, I don't want to take any steps." TJ shook his head, trying to remove the thousands of thoughts piercing through his mind. His inadequacies. His failures. The rasping sound of his sister's final breaths. *Oh God.* He clutched his stomach. The smells in the corridor were too strong. The lights too bright. Everything was too much and yet, if he left, then that was it.

Done.

Over.

"I can't, Daz." He shoved to his feet, stumbled out the door, and raced down the hall, ignoring Freddie's frantic shout and his Mom's, "Let him go."

He glared at Antonacci who stood guard by the elevator and lifted his hand palm up, preempting any conversation. The elevator dinged. He rode down and then walked out to bright blue skies. Why wasn't it raining? Shouldn't the skies be cloudy? The humidity sucked the air out of his lungs. Sweat dripped down his back and built on his forehead, and he squinted against the sun's glare.

Cupping a hand over his brow, he caught sight of a dive bar's sign down the road. Then he let one foot step in front of the other until he sank onto a rickety wooden barstool and asked the bartender to pour him something that would burn all the way down his dry, empty throat until it completely saturated his broken heart.

The wizened blonde with the name, "Randall" tattooed across her chest, tipped some Jim Beam into a glass. "Honey, drinking doesn't erase the pain. Just makes it worse, but hell, I'll take your money. Don't make no never mind to me." She looked him up and down. "You're too handsome to be so sad. Not only that," she tapped her bottom lip, eyes squinting behind her bright red bifocals. "You seem familiar, you famous or something?"

"Sure, I'm famous. Does that mean I can drink for free?" He dropped his phone on the bar's sticky top, ignored all the text notifications, downed the contents of the glass, and then tapped a finger against its rim. "Keep 'em coming."

SIXTEEN

"I don't like this part." TJ fiddled with a loose string on his ripped jeans.

Freddie narrowed his eyes, then slipped off his black jacket and folded it carefully against the arm of the chair.

"Preparing for battle, Daz?"

"Essentially, yes, but you put me in the war-zone."

TJ nodded. "I did yeah, I believe I've said I'm sorry a few times."

Freddie grunted. "That you have."

Surrounded by beige and white furniture in the cancer care's lounge, Freddie stopped pacing for a moment and faced the gathered troops. Jared, TJ's assistant plus Drake and Kim were seated at a round table, trying to locate their errant lead singer before everyone else on Apollo's team found out. The more people that knew, the more likely a leak would hit the press. They'd alerted Bruce—kind of hard not to when Antonacci had watched TJ leave. That thought sent fire through his blood again. He'd yelled at the security guard for just letting TJ walk out the building until Sheila dragged him back into the room. TJ had one of the most recognized faces in the world, and the stupid man had just let him go. Why did they pay all this money for a security team that essentially didn't keep them safe?

He grumbled under his breath and started pacing again. After TJ had bailed on them, he'd comforted Sheila and Megan as best he could, and then he'd helped them finalize arrangements for Emily. He was using Sheila's phone because Bruce still had his. The horrific memory of Emily struggling through those final breaths still played on a loop in his mind. His psycho ex had left him threatening messages. He'd cancelled his visit with his mom for tonight. He was tired, hungry, and irrationally irritated with everyone and everything so this mad search was the last thing he wanted to do. He should just say, screw it and let TJ come back on his own.

"What an absolute selfish jerk!" Kim threw her empty coffee cup into the recycling bin. "I'm gonna punch him in the face."

"He's hurting," Drake mumbled.

"Quit sticking up for him." Kim shot back. "He's always doing this, running off and doing stupid crap and stressing everyone out."

"You're both right." Freddie heaved a long sigh. "We all know TJ's an asshole. He'll get drunk, high or whatever and then post his idiotic behavior on social media. Bruce will track him down, and we'll deal with the fallout."

He'd known TJ would lose his mind when Emily died, but he'd believed they would grieve together. Obviously he'd given a bit more faith than was warranted. How dare TJ run off after giving him all those relationship speeches. Kim wasn't the only one thinking violent thoughts. Only he'd punch TJ, then kiss him, and then punch him again. Though punching people wasn't right...or nice, and he'd hate to think he was turning into an abusive person, so maybe he'd just throw things. Not nice things, but like stuffed animals. Yeah, he'd throw those at TJ. And what in the hell was he thinking about right now? "I think I'm losing my mind. You guys don't even know."

Kim patted his arm. "S'okay, boo. TJ does that to a person."

Jared glanced up from his phone. "How are Sheila and Megan doing?"

The kid was on his phone even more than TJ. He could win Gold medals in both texting and watching YouTube. A nice looking kid, clean-cut, brown hair and brown eyes. He always wore khaki's and polo's in muted colors. Their stylists needed to give him a makeover like right now.

Freddie sighed, his mind was all over the place if he was thinking of stuffed animals and replacing Jared's gray shirts with more vibrant purples or maybe even a nice maroon. "What did you ask? Oh right, well...the doctor prescribed a sleeping pill so Sheila could rest, and I asked my Mom to take them groceries. She'll get there and organize everything in her usual manner. Megan was focusing on taking care of Sheila, so...yeah...that's how they're doing."

"I love your Mom." Kim piped up. "She makes awesome double-chocolate chip cookies."

"Those would be amazing right now." Freddie's mouth watered at the thought.

"How are you holding up?" Drake stood and squeezed his shoulder.

"Not great."

"We'll find him."

"Yeah." Freddie bit his bottom lip. "TJ will turn up. He always does. It...it's just...hard when..." *I need him.* He shook his head. "It's just hard."

Drake nodded. "I know."

Jared tossed his phone onto the table. "I think you guys are being a bit hard on him. He just lost his sister. He cancelled the tour. You wouldn't believe the weight he's had to carry the past couple days. So, maybe back off a little."

Kim narrowed her eyes and opened her mouth.

"Kim." Freddie cut off what would surely be the dressing-down of the century and turned to face Jared. The kid had always seen TJ with rose-colored glasses, but he did have a point. "Jared, we love TJ, always have, but his behavior affects us all."

"Kind of like *your* choices affect the band cancelling shows."

Freddie gasped and took a small step back.

"That's out of line." Drake held up a hand. "TJ tends to forget he's not a one man show. We've *all* worked hard the past couple days. And do not blame Freddie for Kyle's behavior. That's harsh."

Jared shrugged, shoved out of his chair, and then walked over to the candy machine.

"Freddie," Drake started.

"No. He's right." He took a deep breath. "I'm sorry about Kyle. I'm sorry about my hand. I'm sorry I let you guys down. Maybe I should've—"

"Don't." Kim wrapped her tiny body around him, squeezing his middle. "Don't blame yourself. Come on. Let's go find some chocolate, and we'll grab a notebook from somewhere and work on finishing that song we started last week, remember?"

"Okay. Yeah, sure." He'd grab onto this lifeline with both hands. Music would always get him through. "Thank you." He kissed Kim's cheek. "Let's go talk to Jared so he'll quit pouting by the vending machine. I think I'll just get a plain chocolate bar."

"Bruce will find TJ soon enough. Don't worry, okay?" Kim tugged him along.

Jared faced them when they stopped at his side. The kid had his phone plastered to his ear. "Um...Freddie."

"Yeah." His stomach dropped as the kid's tone did not bode well.

"Pepper's on the line. She says your Dad has been calling everyone trying to reach you."

"Oh." And that news didn't help his stomach at all. "Did she say what he wanted?"

"No, just that he was upset he couldn't get a hold of you."

"Are you speaking to Pepper now?"

"Yes."

"May I speak to her?"

"Sure." Jared handed over his phone.

Freddie pressed the cell to his ear as he walked away from Jared and Kim. "Hi Pepper, what's up?"

"Hey Freddie, how's your hand?"

"I'm not sure." He frowned, unclear why she'd mention his hand when so many other things were more relevant right now. "So, Jared said my Dad's been looking for me?"

"Yeah, he's upset you haven't been answering your phone and is accusing us of blocking his calls."

"Huh? Well, I'm sorry about that. I'll...uh...I'll call him now. Again, tell everyone I'm sorry...for him and for...you know...the tour. We'll get back to work as soon as we can."

"It's all right, Freddie. Take the time you need. I'm handling everything here."

He smiled. "You're an angel."

"Hah! Not hardly."

She hung up after that, and Freddie pressed a hand against his pounding heart. What did his father want? And why was he, a grown man, still worried he was in trouble? He took a deep breath, considered diving right in and calling his dad, but used Jared's phone to call his mom instead.

His Dad answered, "Who's this?"

Oh crap. "Uh...Dad, it's me, Freddie."

"What's going on? Why are you calling from this number? Your mother was expecting you tonight and you cancel?"

"I know. I'm sorry." Freddie slumped into the closest chair. The wood frame was the only thing keeping him from crumpling onto the floor. "I did call her."

"What's going on with your band? The news says you've cancelled all your shows. You can't do things like that, Freddie. People paid good money to see you and you just left them high and dry."

"Dad, maybe you don't know this, but Emily died today. So while, yes, people did pay good money, right now, family comes first."

"Is that so? And which family is that, because it sure isn't this one."

Freddie stared at his hand. His broken hand. Enough was enough. His quiet acceptance of his father's mental abuse would end today. He would not allow this man to berate him for standing by a family who'd accepted him unconditionally. "Emily was like a sister to me. And instead of asking how I'm doing, how her family is doing, you're calling to chastise me for something that doesn't matter. That's absolutely cold and unfeeling." He blinked back tears. "I don't need your lectures on how to handle my job. Death trumps everything, and I will not be made to feel bad for taking time to grieve."

"I *will* lecture you on your job. I'm your father. You can't just cancel on people, and if you can't even take my criticism, you'll never survive in your industry."

"I'm ending this conversation because I can't say anything that'll change your opinion of me."

"Sure take the easy way out. End the conversation because you can't handle when I give you a little truth."

"I'm over your truths." Freddie gritted his teeth. "And I've been handling a hell of a lot from you for years."

"Don't use that language with me."

"*Language?*" Freddie barked out a harsh laugh. "You're the one with horrible language."

"Call your Mom when you get some sense."

And then he hung up.

Freddie sucked in a breath, stared at the phone for a moment, and then dropped to the floor and burst into tears.

Small arms wrapped around him and Kim's sweet voice whispered soothing words into his ear. "It's okay, Freddie. It's okay."

He wasn't sure how long she held him before Drake took her place, propping him against his strong shoulder, handing him tissue after tissue.

But Drake's comforting embrace wasn't the one he wanted. And though he felt bad about that because his friends were here and actually trying, yet they weren't enough. Emily was gone. TJ was gone. His father was a raging jerk. His hand hurt, his nose throbbed, and his eyes felt like someone had rubbed them with gritty sandpaper.

He stared at the wad of napkins at his feet and blew his nose with the final tissue from the box on Drake's lap. "Sorry about that."

"No problem. You're allowed to cry."

"I really need to hit my drums. I miss them."

"I know what you mean," Drake squeezed his shoulder.

"My stupid hand though."

"Hey, it'll all get better. Everything in time. It'll be good again."

He sniffed. "You think."

"I know."

Kim crouched down in front of him and passed over a chocolate bar. "How about you start feeling better with this?"

"Chocolate cures all, right?"

"Of course." Kim smiled.

He unwrapped the chocolate and plopped a piece in his mouth. The smooth sugar melted against his tongue, and his stomach growled as if saying, give me more. He took a big bite and spoke as he chewed, knowing it was ill mannered but so hungry he didn't care. "Any word on TJ?"

Against his cheek, he felt Drake's chest rise as his band mate took a deep breath.

"Yeah, he just posted on Instagram."

Freddie straightened and swallowed down the mass of chocolate in his mouth. "Let me see."

Kim handed over her phone and pushed play on the queued up video.

TJ stood inside a darkly lit bar, inviting everyone out that evening for a free concert because he'd forgot his wallet. He'd tagged Kim and Drake, and asked them to bring his guitar.

Freddie gripped the phone in his hand. "He's lost his mind. This is the stupidest thing he's ever done. He'll get swarmed."

Kim winced as she took back her phone. "We better get there, yeah?"

Freddie shot to his feet. "Jared!"

"What?"

Freddie jumped because the kid was literally on the other side of Kim. He just hadn't noticed. *Brilliant, Davis.* "Oh, sorry. Could you please call Jackson?"

"Already on it." He wiggled his phone back and forth.

"Well, looks like you're earning your Gold medal after all."

"What?" Jared arched a brow.

"Nothing." Freddie turned to Kim and Drake. "Let's go save TJ's ass. Again."

Kim grinned. "I call dibs on punching his lights out."

Freddie shook his head. "If he's still in one piece then, yeah, feel free to knock out all his lights. Or maybe not, I think we've all had a enough violence, yeah?"

Kim frowned but she nodded. "Sorry, Fred."

"No, it's all right." He took a deep breath, his first full intake of air since TJ had walked out of Emily's room. Yet, a slither of unease crept down his spine over all the potential hazards TJ could encounter when opening himself up to the public like this.

As he followed Jared out the sliding glass doors of the cancer center, Freddie considered how vulnerable they *all* were right now. No security team to protect them, and they were walking into a potentially uncontrolled environment. TJ's very public statement would bring out all the crazy fans.

Blinking against the sun's glare, Freddie nodded his hello to Jackson as Jared slipped into the front passenger seat.

Jackson smiled and opened the back door. Freddie thanked him then swiped a hand against his sweaty brow as he slid into the back-seat of the air-conditioned sedan with Drake and Kim.

Blocking out his band mates voices, he stared out the window. His heart pounding over the thought that one fan existed who was crazier than all the rest—a fan that now knew exactly where to find him.

SEVENTEEN

"AND THIS NEXT PART IS JUST ANOTHER CHERRY ON TOP OF A *rotted cupcake.*" *Freddie shook his head.*

"Ah, yes, TJ Hardcastle has a drunken breakdown in a Chicago dive-bar."

Freddie shoved TJ's shoulder. "You're such a dick."

"You like my dick."

Freddie cleared his throat before meeting Ms. Burris's gaze. "Let's move on. We're finally getting to the rough stuff, and my wine glass is sadly empty."

SUFFERING THROUGH THE THICK HEAT AND TRYING VERY HARD to maintain his smile, Freddie posed for pics with the Apollo fans gathered outside the run-down bar. TJ had picked a real doozy. The gravel parking lot had potholes the size of Lake Michigan, and the neon Budweiser sign in the window had a blinking B.

With Drake, Kim, and Jared at his side, Freddie trudged through the gathered devotees that barely let him pass even though he was kinda critical to the whole concert happening. Yet, TJ Hard-castle was inside and that was all that mattered to those who believed the lead singer *was* the entire band. Not that Freddie had ever cared, but today the idea pissed him off. He chalked that up to being cranky, hungry, and overall just heartbroken.

Once they made their way through the front door, Freddie followed Kim as Drake and Jared surged forward. Packed like sardines was an understatement. Surely this crowd was breaking at least twenty fire codes.

Drake and Jared twisted past a veritable mix of patrons, ranging from young women in shorts and tanks to what was likely this bar's regular crowd, older men in faded jeans, worn T-shirts, and scuffed work boots.

"This is insane." Kim shouted over the din. "Can you see TJ?"

"Yes, he's just up ahead, standing on what looks like a little stage." Freddie had caught sight of TJ the second he'd stepped into the bar. He'd developed a type of radar for the man, which had been unfortunate when TJ was across the room flirting or following some random guy into one of the concert's backstage rooms.

Freddie shook those thoughts from his mind as, once again, someone bumped him and spilled alcohol on his new shoes. His glorious maple-colored wing tip Oxford's were custom-made, and TJ was buying him a new pair. Maybe two new pairs for his troubles.

Kim continued to barrel through the crowd. Freddie swore he could see the steam pouring out of her ears. He certainly caught her mumblings, which were quite creative descriptions of what she'd do to TJ once she got ahold of him. Some were very impressive, he particularly liked the one where she'd wrap the mic cord around his balls and then shove everything up his ass.

When a loud holler went up in the crowd, Freddie half-jumped out of his skin. He glanced at the stage. Drake was now beside TJ, his brow furrowed, hands gesturing wildly, and words spilling out his mouth that didn't look very friendly.

Taking in the crowds raw-edginess, Freddie reconsidered his plan to yank TJ from the bar and bolt out the back door—if this place even had a back door. When had he become such a venue-snob? Hmm...he'd have to consider that after he showered, ate, slept, and basically did anything else but what he was doing right now.

All these people pressing against him were freaking him out. He couldn't escape easily. Bruce was on his way, so they'd have some level of security. But at this point, if these people didn't get a concert of some sort, there'd be hell to pay.

Behind him, someone shouted his name.

He froze.

That voice sounded a lot like Kyle's.

Once again, a male voice hollered what sounded like his name.

Freddie ducked then slowly glanced over his shoulder, but he couldn't see Kyle anywhere.

Maybe his fears were making him paranoid, but that voice sure sounded like Kyle's.

"Freddie, what are you doing?"

Shrieking out a curse, he pressed a hand against his thrumming heart. "Jesus, Kim. You scared me."

"What are you hanging back here for? We need to get up there with Drake."

"I thought I heard someone yelling my name."

She frowned and glanced around. "Yeah, it's probably someone wanting a picture or something."

"But it was a man's voice." Freddie sucked in a breath and blew it out slowly.

"Well, everyone does know you're gay. Doesn't surprise me someone is trying to get your attention."

"You think so?"

"Uh...yeah. You're gorgeous. It's annoying. Now let's go. I don't have time to feed your ego." She grabbed his arm and tugged him forward.

Though his sixth sense was screaming to vacate the premises, and not only save his high-dollar shoes but to save himself, he stumbled along after her.

Their lead singer was standing by Drake but surrounded by girls who held out cocktail napkins and pens. Others stood in front of TJ with their phones in hand, one arm held out and their smiles wide as they snapped pictures. Some were pawing his arms and every other body part they could touch. In other words—the usual.

TJ did a double take when he saw Freddie and then practically knocked over two girls trying to get to him. "Freddie! Here he is." He wrapped him in a hug. "Glad you're here. I needed you. I tried to call and you wouldn't answer."

He smelled like the inside of a bourbon barrel and every other word out of his whiskey-scented mouth was a bit slurred.

"Dang it, TJ." Freddie shoved against his chest. "How are we supposed to play for all these people?"

"What?" TJ blinked and leaned a little heavier against him. "But you were supposed to bring the stuff." He gaze dropped to Freddie's lips. "Are you pouting? I love it when you pout. Makes me want to do things to your mouth."

"Oh, my God. You need to stop." Freddie held up a hand between them before turning to Drake. "He needs coffee."

"What *stuff* were we supposed to bring?" Kim glared at TJ with both hands on her hips. "We don't walk around with our instruments on our backs. What the hell were you thinking? We can't play here, and all these people are going to murder us because of it." She smacked the side of his head. "What's wrong with you?"

Drake took Kim's hand, likely so she wouldn't hit TJ again. "We know what's wrong with him, but we won't get into that right now because, you're right, we need to figure out something because these fans will turn rabid soon."

As if Drake had seen into the future, a couple people started yelling at them to play, using not-so-nice tones, more like demanding them to play. Couldn't they see that no one had any freaking instruments? Freddie breathed deep, wasn't the fans fault, but seriously? Their entitlement blew his mind sometimes.

Jared hopped up on stage, phone in hand. "Bruce is outside. He and his men are working their way in now."

"Jared!" TJ beamed at his assistant. "Hey, Freddie, Jared's here."

"That's nice, TJ. Thank you for that news flash." Freddie rolled his eyes. "We can't leave without causing a riot so TJ *is* going to sing. We will do three songs then Bruce can get us out of here. Now, Jared, go get TJ some coffee, and we'll see if we can't sober him up a little."

"My pretty, Dazzler." TJ dropped his forehead on Freddie's shoulder. "I'm so happy you're here."

Freddie heaved a long sigh. "Please note that in your drunk mind for later. I *am* here."

TJ eased back, brow furrowed. "I know. I just said, I'm happy you're here."

Drake ran a hand through his hair. "Sweet baby Jesus, we're all gonna die."

Freddie passed an overly-smiley TJ to Drake then turned to Kim. "Can you do a quick mic test? We'll brace TJ on a barstool. I can hold him up while I sing with him, and we'll give these fans something at least."

Kim nodded then hustled over to test the mic.

Ignoring shouts from the crowd and the girls hovering nearby snapping pics, Freddie held TJ's face between his hands. "Focus for a second, we'll sing. Then I'm taking you home, and once you sober up, we're having a long talk about consequences to stupid actions."

"I'm sorry, Daz. I just...I couldn't handle it. I couldn't." TJ shook his head then dropped his chin and stared at the floor. "I wanted to be strong for everyone but I just couldn't."

"We'll have this discussion later. Right now, we need to deal with this crowd."

"But I want to go home with you." He flashed a grin at Freddie and gently gripped his hand, swinging it back and forth between them.

Freddie couldn't help but grin back, and a tiny spark of sympathy poked through because TJ seemed so childlike and help-less. Yet, the crowd was now chanting and pounding on the tables. Groups of girls were close enough to bump them off this matchbox-sized stage, so he had to put everything aside and deal with this moment.

He wouldn't think about how he'd trusted TJ and been let down. Plus, he wasn't in the mindset to figure everything out right now. "TJ, I'd like to go home too, but you posted that you would sing and so well, you're going to sing. Sober up, we're doing this."

Freddie caught a glimpse of Jared carefully making his way over with a white cup of steaming hot coffee. In a glass mug. "What in the world?" He pressed forward to help guide Jared to the stage before he suffered stage four burns. "Be careful." He took the cup from Jared and handed it to TJ. "Drink all of this."

TJ met his gaze. "Right, right, I'm sorry, Freddie. I'll fix this."

Freddie nodded and glanced out over the crowd who were now chanting, Apollo.

Kim tapped Freddie's shoulder. "The mic is as ready as it's gonna be. Good luck with that relic from the 70's."

Drake brought over a stool and settled TJ onto it.

TJ's eyes were closed as he sipped the coffee, and Freddie was half worried he'd pass out before they even started.

TJ opened his eyes again and met Freddie's gaze once more. "Here take this." He handed Freddie his empty coffee cup and turned to the crowd. "Thanks everybody for coming out tonight."

Freddie marveled at how quickly TJ could turn on his role as lead singer of Apollo. Still, the man had partied a lot in the past couple years, so his tolerance level was probably pretty high.

TJ basically shouted into the crowd for a minute then turned to Freddie. "Come here, Daz." He waved him over. "Me and Freddie, we go way back. Like to the very beginning, did you guys know that? Anyway, this mic sucks so he's gonna add his voice to mine, and we'll see if we can sing a couple songs for ya."

Freddie wished he'd downed a couple whiskey shots. Normally he hid behind his drums. He wiped his shaky hands against his pants, trying to focus on TJ and not the rabid fans basically inches from his body. No layers existed between him and the crowd tonight, and honestly, he hated how unsafe he felt. Hopefully Kyle wasn't out there, preparing to rush the stage and break his other hand.

TJ bumped him with his elbow. "Hey? You with me?"

Freddie nodded and swallowed hard.

"He's a dreamer, my Freddie. Anyway, he writes these songs so hopefully he can keep me on track. It's been a horrible day, and I just want to sing then go home and fuck."

The crowd roared with laughter and a few people offered up their services.

Freddie turned to TJ, placing a hand over the mic. "What the hell, TJ? They're already out of control. Quit instigating them."

TJ just laughed then leaned closer. "Don't worry. It's only you I want to fuck."

"I will literally murder your face off." Freddie eased back

because he felt heat rise in a place it shouldn't be rising. He was still so angry at this man and having an erection in front of all these people was ridiculous. Eyes narrowed, he pressed a finger against TJ's lips. "You have no idea of my level of pissedoffness and you just keep adding layers. I was at red, but now I'm beyond that to some level of red heretofore unknown."

TJ licked his lips, gaze on Freddie's mouth before he sighed. "Stop using big words. We've got songs to sing."

Freddie brought his hands up and for just a moment considered choking the absolute life out of the man. Instead, he remembered he was against violence and grabbed the mic instead. He hummed the opening riff to, "*Better Days.*"

TJ added his sultry voice so Freddie handed the mic over.

They sang three songs together during which Bruce and his men had made their way to the front of the stage. Jared, Kim, and Drake were no longer anywhere to be seen so Bruce must've got them out somehow.

After the third song, TJ tried to say goodnight, but the crowd surged forward so to placate them, he sang one more.

While singing the second verse, Freddie caught sight of about six cops trying to usher people out.

Shouts started, as fans voiced their opinion over the police making them leave.

And then like a scene out of an old western movie, one person shoved another.

That person shoved back which bumped someone else.

Beer flew through the air.

Screams of outrage rumbled through the crowd as the shoving intensified.

All they needed now was a piano playing, "The Entertainer."

Bruce hopped up on the stage, hooked both TJ and Freddie in his beefy arms, and then rushed them toward the back door.

Sounds of breaking glass mixed with the roar of angry fans, fights, and policemen struggling to regain order.

A mass of bodies slipped out the door with them, shoving them forward.

Freddie tried to glance over his shoulder to make sure no one was being trampled but Bruce snapped at him to keeping moving.

Two cop cars surrounded the black sedan Jackson had been using to usher them from place to place.

A couple news vans were parked on the other side of the police cars.

As he made his way over to Jackson, Freddie ignored the reporters as they shouted questions. The cameramen at their sides were catching everything on tape. *Great, the publicity team will just love this.*

With the back door barely open, they tumbled inside, and Jackson started moving forward.

"Fucking hell, Jackson," TJ groused. "I didn't even have the door shut."

"Mr. Hardcastle, I know you are not using that language with me."

"Sorry, Jackson."

"That's better. Now, I know that I don't have to tell you that you done messed up good."

"Always telling me like it is, aren't ya?"

"Someone has to. Old Jackson ain't one of your yes men."

"And I thank God for that every day."

"Don't be trying to sweet talk me now. You save all that sugar for that boy there with you." He crept along slowly as people bombarded the car, making them rock a little.

"We're in for it now." Jackson huffed out a sigh. "Water bottles are in the cooler at your feet. Drink up now."

"Thanks, Jackson."

Freddie took a bottle, handed one to TJ and then drank. Though water spilled down his chin as his hand was shaking like crazy.

"That was scary as hell." TJ slumped against the seat.

Freddie was so angry he didn't trust himself to speak. This whole situation could have been avoided if TJ wasn't a selfish ass that ran away from his troubles like a big stupid jerk. "Yes, TJ, it *was* scary as hell. Thanks so much for adding that insightful comment to my life." He snapped his seatbelt in place and sipped from his half-empty bottle.

"I'm so tired." TJ plopped his head on Freddie's shoulder

"Get your sweaty head off of me." Freddie shoved him away, wiping his now sweat-laden hands on his pants. "Buckle your seat belt."

TJ groaned, but straightened and locked the seatbelt over his chest. "You're so mean to me."

"Given the fact that I don't advocate violence to solve problems, I'd like it noted that I'm trying very hard not to absolutely lose my calm right now and just punch you in the face. I'm so angry for so many reasons, but I don't want to discuss it because I'll say things I can't take back."

TJ was quiet for a moment. Then his phone started pinging.

Freddie glared. "Turn that thing off, please. That sound grates on my nerves like nothing else on this earth." He glanced out the window, grateful they had moved away from the bar's crush of people and were now driving past the cancer treatment center. He turned away.

"Gosh, Daz. Taking your anger out on my phone. It's an inanimate object. That's so not cool."

"I do *not* find you humorous right now."

TJ sighed. "I'm sorry, okay. I messed up. Surprise, surprise, TJ Hardcastle messed up. He let you down. You've been expecting it all along so I don't know why you're so mad right now."

"That's just amazing reasoning. Good job."

"I couldn't breathe in there, Fred. I ran, yeah, and I'm sorry but I don't know that I'd change what I did. I needed some space."

"Well that's really great, real mature, especially given that we could have died in that bar just now!" Freddie sucked in a breath, because he'd basically just yelled in TJ's face. "Now could you please just shut up? When I'm ready to talk to you, I will, but right now, *I* can't breathe, and on top of that, I'm starving, I'm exhausted, I'm scared, hurt, soaked with sweat and beer and whatever other just...fluids. And oh yes, my shoes are ruined. Thanks for that, by the way." He glanced down at his shoes, now stained with various liquids and another surge of anger raced through his veins. "But guess what? *I* can't run, not like you did. I have to stay in this car because you put our band and me in a dangerous situation. So please just give me some god damned quiet." He pounded a fist against his knee, crying now because that's what he did when he was upset, which infuriated him further. His eyes were already sore from crying over Emily, not to mention all the smoke in that bar. Wasn't that supposed to be illegal now? He shook his head and wiped his nose on his sleeve. "Gross! God, I just want this day to be over."

TJ held out his hand. "Freddie, please."

"No," Freddie shrank back against the door. "Just no. Leave me alone."

TJ stared at him for a moment before releasing a raspy breath. "Okay, Daz. Okay."

Freddie leaned forward to ask Jackson if he had any tissues and to see where they were going. But then his entire body shot forward, his head banged against the back of the passenger seat before his seatbelt snapped him back into place.

Stunned and his chest beginning to ache from the seatbelt's hold, Freddie rubbed a hand against the back of his neck. "What in the world?"

He glanced over at TJ who was wide-eyed and hissing out a breath as he stared out the back window.

"Hey, you okay?" Freddie tried to look back too, but with the twinge of pain shooting down his back, he decided not moving might be best. "I think...I think we got rear-ended."

TJ blinked. "Fuck, man." He pulled his seatbelt away from his chest. "That hurt."

Jackson moaned from the front seat.

"Oh my God, Jackson, you okay?" Freddie bit down hard on his bottom lip. His neck ached, but he unbuckled and scooted forward a little to check on their driver.

His door flew open and a big hand reached inside.

Freddie shrieked and scrabbled away.

"Holy shit." TJ roared from beside him.

Kyle's ominous form crouched in the open door. "Gotcha."

Freddie yelped as he was dragged across the seat and set on his feet outside the vehicle.

Kyle had a crooked grin in place and an odd glint in his eyes. "Good to see you again, Freddie."

"What are you doing here?" Freddie swallowed hard. "Did...did you just hit us?"

"I told you I'd find you." He wrapped Freddie in his arms and hauled him over to a big pickup truck.

The truck's front end was pressed against the back of their sedan.

"Wait." Freddie squirmed, his knocked-around brain finally catching up with everything going on around him. He shoved against Kyle, trying to break free of his grip. "Stop. I'm not going anywhere with you."

Kyle grinned, set him back on his feet, and then pulled a K-Bar from his back pocket. "Don't make me use this. I said, we're leaving and I mean it. I already dented my truck for you, so let's go." Jaw clenched, he grabbed Freddie's bad hand and squeezed.

No! This will not happen again. Tears sprang to his eyes, but he shoved away, wincing as pain shot through his hand and his whiplashed neck. "Please, Kyle, this is insane."

A car door slammed, making Freddie jump.

Kyle's eyes narrowed as he glanced over Freddie's shoulder. "Let's go." He yanked on his arm and pulled him forward.

"What the fuck are you doing?" TJ stood beside the back of the car, hands braced on his hips.

They were blocked from each other due to the truck being pressed up against the sedan.

"TJ, he's got a knife."

TJ grunted but didn't look away from Kyle. "Bruce and his crew are right behind us. I'd take off if I were you."

Kyle chuckled. "Yeah, they won't get far with slashed tires."

"God, I really hate you." TJ cracked his knuckles and then nodded. "Well then, I guess it's up to me."

Freddie shook his head, pressing his throbbing hand against his chest. "No, TJ, whatever you're thinking, just no."

"He's not taking you anywhere."

"TJ, please. It's okay. I'll be okay." He was crying now and edging his way closer to the back of the sedan. "Don't do anything stupid."

TJ hopped up, slid over the sedan's trunk, and then shoved Freddie behind him.

Kyle flipped the knife up in the air and caught it. "Fine, Hardcastle. You think you can stop me? Go ahead and try."

It was one thing to threaten him, but having the man purposefully track him down and now stand here with a knife and threaten TJ, well, enough was enough.

Freddie lunged forward, tipping Kyle off balance.

He grunted then shifted.

TJ yelled some sort of crazed battle cry and swung at Kyle.

Kyle slipped to the side then swung around, knife in hand.

Freddie screamed and shot forward, shoving TJ out of the way.

A blow landed against his upper arm.

TJ tumbled to the ground, and Freddie fell on top of him unable to brace himself so they landed hard.

His arm started to sting and throb.

He sucked in a breath and glanced over.

The blade was stuck in his arm. The remaining silver glinting a little under the streetlights as if saying, "Tada!"

"No, no, no." Freddie blinked then looked again. Yep, the knife was still buried in his arm, blood starting to seep from where it was embedded in his flesh.

His head spun and red and blue lights flashed across his eyes.

A loud sound like a siren, erupted from somewhere behind him.

TJ scurried out from underneath him. "Freddie? Hey, you okay?"

Then TJ was gone, lifted up in the air and thrown somewhere.

Kyle dropped to his knees beside Freddie and yanked out the blade.

Freddie released a scream unlike anything he'd ever heard before as fiery-pain seared down his arm. Dizzy and on the verge of throwing up, he blinked again, trying to make sense of the chaos around him. "Oh my God, that fucking hurt, you asshole!"

Someone said Kyle's name very loudly, as if from a megaphone.

Freddie groaned and turned on his side, holding a hand against his bloody arm. Would he bleed out here? Die in a puddle of blood on this Chicago street?

Kyle cursed as he rose to his feet, lifting his hands in the air.

"W-what? What are you doing?" Sweat trickled down the side of his face as Freddie glanced around for TJ. "Where...TJ! Where are you? What did you do with him?" Freddie kicked out at Kyle's legs, but the man just stood there, glaring ahead, arms raised.

"Drop the weapon." A megaphone voice ordered.

Oh, the megaphone is a cop.

Freddie tensed. He was in the middle of a standoff. They'd probably start shooting, and he'd die from multiple holes in his body —bullets, knife wounds, and whatever else. And why wasn't Kyle dropping the knife? Was he insane? Oh, yeah, that's right, he was. Freddie giggled, a nervous giggle. In pain, sweating, scared out of his freaking mind, and not sure where in the hell TJ had gone, let alone Jackson, he simply laughed until he cried. "I am so over you, Kyle. I hope you rot in jail. Drop the stupid knife before you get us all killed, you idiot!"

He pulled his hand away from his wound. It was dark red, sticky, and dripping with blood. Oh, fuck, there went his head, spinning around and around. He released a long breath, and tried to pretend he didn't smell the blood pouring out his arm. Should he take off his shirt to stem the bleeding like they did in action movies? Had the knife hit some major arm artery?

Another shout from the megaphone.

"Oh my God! Have some sense for once." He glared up at Kyle, unable to stop the words spilling forth. His anger had taken over, and he honestly didn't care if Kyle kicked him to shut him up. He'd been kicked before. So he'd survive. "And another thing I want to say... you suck in bed. Like so bad. And your dick is tiny. Like a ferrets because ferrets have small dicks, I bet. I don't know for sure, but yeah, you have a ferret dick!"

He heard someone laugh.

Kyle stared down at him with narrowed eyes.

"Listen up, ferret dick." The megaphone voice sounded more amused than they should be at the moment. "We will shoot. Last chance, drop the knife."

"Drop it! What's wrong with you!" Freddie shook his head then winced because that hurt his stupid neck again.

Kyle opened his hand, and the knife slipped from his bloody fingers.

Freddie yipped and edged away as the blade landed right in front of his face.

He blinked and then four cops were pressing Kyle face down on the pavement, arms locked behind his back.

Kyle met his gaze.

Freddie shot him the finger, because yeah, he was down again, but he'd fought back this time. He'd been strong and protected someone he loved. "See, you psychotic jerk. I'm *not* yours, never was, never will be. Stupid ferret dicked jerk."

The cops led Kyle away and then a handsome boy in blue crouched at Freddie's side. "Mr. Davis, it's okay now. Kyle and his ferret dick will be locked up for a long time."

"You think you're funny but you're not, because he does in fact have a tiny dick, that's all I was saying."

"Yes." The cop sucked in his lips, likely fighting a grin. "We got that." He winked.

"Could you stop flirting with me? I'm dying here. God, what's wrong with you?"

"Well." The cop mused, tapping a finger against his lip. "I know what's *not* wrong with me...*I* don't have a ferret dick."

Freddie groaned and just let his head rest against the pavement. "I hate you all."

EIGHTEEN

TJ was laughing so hard he was crying.

Ms. Burris had picked up on his glee and joined in.

Freddie had left them to their ridiculousness and grabbed a bottle of red from the kitchen. "Let me know when you're finished. And just to be clear, I've become overrun with everything ferret since that day, and don't think I don't know how it all started, Hardcastle. I blame you."

TJ just hooted with laughter.

Freddie rolled his eyes and poured a very large glass of red wine. But he did smile a little, because it was funny.

Mid-afternoon the next day, Freddie shuffled into the hotel's living room area, wearing two different socks, loose sweats, and Drake's even looser sweatshirt.

Drake and Kim were sitting on the couch playing *Mortal Kombat.*

Yawning, Freddie was more awake than he wanted to be as he

plopped into a chair. He winced as he shifted, trying to find a comfortable position. The knife had essentially gone through the flesh of his upper arm, not causing any muscle damage, which was a good thing, because having his fingers mangled was bad enough. While at the hospital last night, they'd rewrapped his fingers, saying they were healing nicely.

A soft double-rap on the door proceeded TJ walking in.

Drake greeted him with a quick, "Hey."

Kim glanced back and forth between TJ and Freddie. "Okay, Drake." She grabbed his arm. "Let's leave these two for a bit, all right?"

Drake nodded then stood and wrapped his arm around her as they left the room.

Freddie rolled his neck side to side, studying TJ from under half-closed lids.

TJ paced in front of the TV. His ass looked amazing in faded jeans and his jawline did look quite lickable with all the scruff. He had a bit of road rash on his right arm, and the light purple circles under his eyes were evidence he hadn't slept well or maybe he hadn't slept at all. Made sense since Freddie had essentially passed out with the help of painkillers last night while TJ and everyone else did whatever needed to be done.

Another punch of guilt hit him in the gut, and he sighed. He'd contributed to TJ's sleeplessness and that wasn't fair. The lead singer thought he had to take care of everyone and everything, but as per usual, he forgot to take care of himself.

All Freddie wanted to do was hold TJ as they both slept. For hours, maybe even days. But he had a lot to say, and then he'd see whether or not they'd end up in bed together or maybe this time, they'd decide they were better off apart.

Freddie cleared his throat—loudly. "All right. I'll start. I'm very sorry for Kyle's actions."

TJ whipped his head in Freddie's direction. "Don't you apologize for that asshole."

Freddie held up a hand. "Please, let me finish. I'm sorry you were a part of that yesterday, and I do thank you for sticking up for me."

TJ's jaw clenched. "Of course, I stuck up for you."

Freddie glared at him.

"Fine, go on." TJ waved a hand in his direction. "But, just, are you okay?"

"No, I'm one big ache."

"Oh. Maybe you should just get some rest then."

"No, we need to have this out."

"If you're sure?"

Freddie nodded. "I'm sure." He took a deep breath and continued. "And I'm also sorry about Emily, so very sorry...but the thing is, I loved her too. We all did. So what you did, after promising you'd try, that...hurt." He waved a hand at his bandaged arm. "The pain from this wound hurts, but with you, I bled from the heart, and I'm still bleeding."

TJ dropped to his knees in front of Freddie. "I'm bleeding too."

"The difference is that I don't create opportunities to bleed."

TJ sighed and took Freddie's hand. "I'm trying to decide if what I practiced saying last night was good enough."

Freddie sniffed. "I can answer that, it's probably not."

"I knew that if I admitted that Emily is...dead...then she would be."

Freddie's heart melted a little as TJ's face crumpled and tears dripped down his cheeks. "Let it out, TJ, because whether you want to accept the truth or not, she's gone." His own tears began to fall as he watched the love of his life collapse against his lap.

TJ's sobs filled the room, and his tears soaked Freddie's pant leg.

Freddie ran his hand through TJ's thick hair, while offering soothing words.

TJ pulled back, wiping his nose. "I'll be back in a second."

He slowly got to his feet and shuffled to the bathroom. He stayed in there long enough for Freddie to worry, but the water had turned on and off a few times.

After everything TJ had put him through, he should just let the man work through his problems on his own, but he couldn't. He didn't trust him right now, but love him? He'd always love him. But love without trust, without dependability, that was the crux of their problems.

TJ came out of the bathroom and dropped beside him again. "Sorry about that."

"You needed to grieve."

TJ pressed his lips together. "I know." He grabbed a beige throw pillow and set it on his lap. He ran a hand back and forth over the velour fabric. "It's just...I never had anything growing up, nothing except this heavy burden that I was supposed to be the man of the house once my dad left. I can't say I would change anything because that doesn't serve any purpose. The only thing that I do wish, and what I'll *always* wish for, is to have Emily back, but I can't have that."

"None of this glosses over the fact that you left the hospital to get drunk, which in turn caused a lot of chaos and just more pain."

"I know." He fisted his hand on top of the pillow. "When she died, I couldn't breathe and having you there made things...you make things real, Daz. I *feel* things with you. And those feelings are always more real and raw. I can drop my guard around you, but in that instance, I wasn't ready to do that." He rubbed the bridge of his nose with his forefinger and thumb, before running a hand over the pillow again. "I'm sorry I let you down. I'm sorry I left you behind. I know I made you promises only to break them, maybe even break us, but I will keep trying. I can't give up now."

"You say things, these nice words spilling out of your mouth, like the sweetest music I've ever heard. But, right now, I'm tired and hurting and still a little bit scared. Yet, above all that, I'm angry because you gave me hope. I believed in you and then you chose to be your usual selfish self. I just...I-I'm not sure how I feel about you right now. And I'm really not sure how I feel about me." Freddie ran a hand over the bandage on his arm. "I've been through a lot too, you know. Maybe I want to be a little selfish this time."

TJ remained quiet for a moment before setting the pillow aside. "All right. I understand, but can you be at my side during Emily's funeral? I-I can't...I can't do it alone."

Freddie closed his eyes and bit down hard on his lower lip. He needed TJ to leave. Needed an escape from those sad eyes. Those drooped shoulders. And that slight shakiness in his voice. He turned and faced TJ again. "Of course I'll be at the funeral, and I'll be there for the band, and nothing has ever stopped me from being there for *you*."

TJ nodded, his lips pulled in tight as he squeezed his eyes shut. When his next words came, they were a harsh whisper, ripped and shredded as they escaped his full lips. "I've always loved you. You're every dream I've ever had, every hope. You're my song. And I'm sorry you never heard me singing, because right now I'm screaming for you. Just you."

Tears falling down his face, Freddie pressed a hand against TJ's chest. "You're my song too, and I want to believe you. But actions speak louder than words. That's what I see. That's what I hear." Freddie pressed his forehead against TJ's solid shoulder. Breathing deep, Freddie ignored that welcoming hint of pine coming from TJ's warm skin.

Easing back an inch, Freddie wiped at the tears on his cheeks, wincing when his arm twinged a little. He wanted to give in, wanted to kiss TJ.

His mouth was right there.

He licked his lips.

TJ's eyes widened.

A whiff of cinnamon beckoned Freddie closer.

They were so close.

So close, he could practically feel the steam building between their bodies.

He could let everything go and just feel. Let those hands touch his body. Let those lips burn against his own. Escape into pleasure... but then what?

Freddie blinked. "I think you should go."

"I will, but I need to say something first." TJ shifted to sit on the coffee table, elbows resting on his knees as he leaned forward and clasped Freddie's left hand. "Remember that play you did in high school? You were the British butler and provided comic relief. Your accent was *so* bad. But you were excited, and had me practice lines with you. We were in your bedroom and out of nowhere, it hit me. You had a pen in your mouth and such an earnest expression on your face, and I thought, he's so beautiful and I love him more than anything. You looked at me and smiled, that indulgent smile, and tilted your head and said, thanks TJ. I thought you were thanking me for loving you, like you'd read my mind."

Freddie remembered that play. Remembered how TJ had helped him practice his few lines over and over as if preparing him for some award-winning role.

"Anyway, I was kinda overwhelmed so I mumbled something and got up and left. Your Dad was at bottom of the stairs, and he said, 'You were up there a long time.' And I said, "yeah.' And he said, 'This is a Christian home,' And I said, 'I'm not sure what you mean.' Then he gets right in my face and says, 'Keep your wickedness away from my son.' I knew exactly what he meant, so I avoided him as much as possible after that."

Freddie sucked in a breath, eyes wide. "I'm so sorry. I didn't know."

TJ nodded and then stood, bracing both hands on his hips. "It's just...even after all the times I've told you to ignore him, well...his words really hit me deep, and I've never forgotten them. It sucks that I let your Dad frame how I've felt about you all these years. I did believe I had to keep my wickedness away from you."

"TJ, that's not true."

"Isn't it? I am pretty fucking wicked." TJ shrugged and gave a half-grin. "I can't change the past couple years, and I don't know that I really want to, because I needed to let loose for a while. I needed to shine in the spotlight. I needed that continual reassurance, the fans, the accolades, the rock star title, because without it, I'm just a wicked kid."

"No, don't say that. You're so much more than that."

"If I am, then why is my wickedness still keeping us apart?" TJ stared down at him for a moment before turning on his heel and walking out the door.

NINETEEN

FREDDIE SIPPED FROM HIS WINE GLASS AND FELT A LITTLE BAD *that no one was laughing now.*

Ms. Burris excused herself for a moment.

TJ watched her leave and then turned and settled onto Freddie's lap. He brushed his hair back before leaning in and kissing him. Softly and slowly. After a long moment, he sat back. "Thinking of that moment hurts."

Freddie placed a hand on TJ's chest, above his beating heart. "I'm here. We're here."

TJ groaned and shifted his hips forward. "And she's still here."

"Not much longer."

"Yeah, cause this is the good part."

"I thought the good part was coming later?"

"Oh there will be coming later."

Freddie rolled his eyes. "That was bad."

"You mean, wicked?"

"Always."

. . .

GRAY CLOUDS FILLED THE SKY AND A SLIGHT BREEZE WHIPPED through the muggy air as Freddie leaned against the car, watching TJ approach. At his feet, puddles of rain from the night before remained on the uneven cemetery roads.

Throughout the late afternoon they'd sat through a semi-private service. Bruce and his team had been busy, keeping unwanted news vans and some well-meaning fans away from the site. They couldn't do much about the drones that had circled overhead earlier though.

Sheila and Megan had left with Drake and Kim. All were on their way to visit with Jackson who was recovering in a very posh hotel room. Right now, he needed a little TLC. They all did.

TJ had remained at the gravesite, hand upon the casket until he'd nodded and watched the workers lower Emily into the ground.

Now, TJ stopped beside him, leaning against the rented black sedan.

The remaining guard, Antonacci stood by the driver's side door, scanning the area for any remaining threats.

After a long moment of quiet, TJ stuffed both hands in the pockets of his black dress pants and sighed. "It's hard being us, isn't it?"

"You want to stop?" Freddie kept his gaze over the gray stones, taking in the pervasive sadness that was par for the course with cemeteries. Perhaps they should be whispering or maybe just leaving in general so that the dead under their feet could be at peace.

That's what he wanted, too. Peace. He'd made a decision. The right decision. The only decision. He'd waited to share it with TJ. Now might be a good time. They needed to start again. Move forward. Forgive.

"I couldn't stop even if I wanted to," TJ said. "We have contracts and people who work for us and five concert dates to reschedule, remember?"

"We do, but we also love it, don't we?" Freddie shrugged. "At least the music part, making it with you, that's what I love."

TJ nodded, biting his lower lip. "I love that too."

"The doctor checked my hand yesterday. Said it's almost ready for therapy." He held it out and twisted it back and forth.

"So, we wait a bit to reschedule. Let me know when you're ready."

"I'm ready." He turned and met TJ's gaze, giving him a soft smile so he'd know he meant something else. Something deeper.

TJ sucked in a breath. "Yeah?"

"Yeah."

"I needed to hear that today."

"Good because, I needed to say it today."

"I'm not easy."

"Well...I'd say you *are* kinda easy." He laughed when TJ lightly jabbed his shoulder. "Thing is TJ, don't leave again. Just don't."

"I didn't leave *you*. I left the situation."

"All right." Freddie nodded. "I'll give you extenuating circumstances this *one* time." He held up a finger between them. "Just once. Don't make me regret giving you another chance.

"Okay, Daz. S'all good then, yeah?"

"Yeah." Freddie stepped between TJ's legs and stared into those caramel-colored eyes. "What are we supposed to do now?"

"Make up sex." TJ grabbed Freddie's hips and pulled him closer.

"Is that so?"

"Yeah, because *I* don't have a ferret dick."

"Been waiting to use that one for a while, haven't you?"

"I have actually. Jesus, Fred, you're on the ground. Cops had their guns drawn, and you're lying there screaming about Kyle's dick."

"I was expressing my feelings, and you know I don't like to cuss."

"I cuss enough for the both of us anyway. And, just so you know, ferret dick is not really a bad word."

Freddie sniffed. "Well, I was in pain and scared out of my mind."

TJ buried his chuckle in Freddie's neck. Then he just stayed there for a while, holding Freddie in his arms.

Other than Antonacci, they were alone in the cemetery now.

Freddie kissed TJ's cheek. "It's finally quiet."

"Maybe out here but not in my head."

"We'll get through the next couple months."

TJ nodded. "But first, make up sex."

"Yeah, let's go see what we can do about that."

TJ bumped their hips together and then took his hand, leading him to the passenger door. He opened it with a flourish. "After you."

Freddie braced his hand at the top of the window. "TJ, about what my father said...I need you to know, you're not wicked."

TJ barked out a laugh. "Um...make up sex *will* be wicked. So, yeah, there's that."

"No, listen, not in the way my father meant. What we feel for each other isn't wicked. Nothing about *us* is wrong."

"Thank you for saying that." TJ pressed a hard kiss to Freddie's lips. "So, you forgive me?"

"I think I do."

"Do you love me?"

"I know I do."

"So after make up sex, maybe we can figure out how to be just TJ and Freddie again?"

"I feel that can be accomplished after make up sex, yes. But only with more sex and then more sex after that."

TJ arched a brow. "I like how you think, Daz."

"Mmm...so, what're we waiting for?" Freddie leaned in to kiss him but a flicker of light caught his eye. Something blinked in TJ's hair. "No way! You have a lightning bug in your hair. Stand still." Freddie pulled it free from TJ's strands.

"I am so epic." TJ laughed and shook his head.

"Right, you called the bug forth to seal your romantic moment. Whatever." Freddie rolled his eyes, because it *was* romantic and perfect and fitting. Not that he'd ever tell TJ that, especially because the bug was now crawling all over his finger giving him the heebie-jeebies. "Uh, TJ, can you get it off my finger, please?"

TJ set the blinking bug onto his palm. "I'm taking this as a good sign."

"Me too."

TJ touched a finger to the bug and it lifted off and flew away. "We won't always have these kinds of moments, Daz, but I promise, I won't leave again."

Freddie nodded as he watched the bug fly off, and considered for a moment that maybe it was a sign from Emily, reminding him of his promise to be TJ's light. A promise he would keep forever.

TWENTY

BACK IN CALIFORNIA

"AND SO, THAT'S THE END." FREDDIE TAPPED HIS DRUMSTICKS against his open palm. "I'm sorry, Ms. Burris. I feel as if we got a little off track at times." He studied the reporter sitting across from him, wondering if perhaps he'd revealed too much.

TJ lounged beside him, thumbs flying across his phone's screen as he texted.

"Thank you for your honesty." Burris lifted both arms above her head and stretched then cut her gaze to him once more. "I almost forgot to ask, what happened to Kyle?" She steadied her laptop on her knee.

"In exchange for assurances that he would start therapy, we agreed to allow him to plead to lesser charges. TJ and Bruce stay up to date on the proceedings more than I do. I just want to be done with Kyle."

TJ cleared his throat. "Let's see, there was attempted murder."

He tapped his cell phone against his open palm. "Assault with a deadly weapon, domestic abuse, attempted kidnapping. I wanted vehicular manslaughter but no one was slaughtered." He shrugged. "I didn't want to go easy on him, but Daz over here has a forgiving heart. I'm grateful for that fact, but Kyle can kiss my ass."

Ms. Burris typed away, adding those sordid details to her story. She really should just look at the court records.

Freddie winced. "I actually hate that he still had to serve time in jail, because I feel like an already violent person in that violent environment will actually come out worse. I just get sick when I think about him in prison."

TJ blew out a long breath. "I agree, Daz, but like I've said before, I just wanted him away from you."

"Yeah, I guess so. It's just awful. All of it." Freddie glanced at his watch, noting it was past dinner time. They'd kept this poor woman all day and had only fed her once. He slapped both hands against his knees. "Well, I think that's about it then. It's late so...we have a guest room if you'd like to stay."

TJ whipped around to stare at him, jaw dropped open in surprise or disgust. Freddie couldn't tell. "What's wrong?"

"Nothing." TJ sighed before setting his phone on the coffee table.

Even though TJ was addicted to the spotlight, he'd always kept their home as a haven away from everything. He didn't like having anyone over but his family and Drake and Kim. He didn't even like it when Jared had to stop by.

"Thank you." The reporter stood and held out her hand. "I appreciate the offer, but I'll just head home. I want to write while everything is fresh in my mind."

Freddie got to his feet and shook her hand.

TJ did the same.

"I'll email you that list of websites and hot-line numbers for the domestic abuse centers." With his drumsticks, Freddie tapped a tune against TJ's chest as Ms. Burris packed her briefcase.

TJ didn't say a word as he was used to being Freddie's toy drum set.

"Do you need any help carrying that?" Freddie motioned to her bag with his drumstick.

"I'm good. Thanks." She set the designer bag on the couch and then stuffed in her computer and papers.

Freddie rubbed the back of his neck and bit his bottom lip.

"What's the matter?" TJ flicked a finger against his lip, stopping him from worrying it

Burris turned and tilted her head to the side. "Was there something else?"

"It's just...I realize our love story would make better magazine copy, but that wasn't the point of this interview. The point is that intimate partner violence occurs in *all* relationships. I don't know why I have to say this but you'd be surprised how many people look at me odd when I say my boyfriend abused me." He ran a hand down his now-wrinkled pink T-shirt. "While I was a victim, yes, I did survive and come out stronger in the end. I *have* stayed in therapy. We're working through more of the mental abuse at this point though, as bruises tend to heal, but hurtful words...well, they take a lot longer. Plus, I'm also learning self-defense maneuvers from one of our security guards."

TJ mumbled something under his breath.

Freddie laughed before rolling his eyes. "TJ gets jealous when I spend time with Beef-A-Roni Antonacci."

"That's *my* nickname for him. Sounds weird coming from your mouth." TJ poked Freddie in the ribs before turning to Ms. Burris. "He's rolling around on mats with the guy. Of course, I'm jealous. That's way too much body contact."

"I take classes, too." Burris nodded. "Jiu-jitsu. It's important to be able to protect yourself."

Freddie instantly sobered. "I agree. And I'd also like to add that I'm well aware that my money gives me options and freedoms that others don't have. I wasn't relying on Kyle for support. We obviously didn't have kids. We weren't married. Ending a relationship can be hard enough, but when someone has you locked in their grip financially, I understand why it's hard to leave." He scratched the back of his neck with the tip of the drumstick. "Many resources do exist though, and I hope that people will read this article and seek help."

TJ wrapped arm around his shoulder and kissed his temple. "They will, Daz." He drew him in for a quick side-hug. "Ms. Burris, I do appreciate you coming here, and I'd like to invite you to sit in during one of the domestic violence group sessions. I think it'd be beneficial to hear what these victims have to say." TJ's jaw clenched. "I was shocked to learn that one very cruel way an abusive partner gains control is through threatening to out their partner. I mean, how big of a dick can a guy be? You don't out someone. Ever."

Freddie frowned as he recalled some of the conversations over the past year. "Right, and some people feel no one will help them because of their sexual orientation or due to how they identify."

"We're also struggling for awareness in law enforcement. Two men fighting is not a norm. Or just how men solve problems. This adds to men not recognizing until too late that they are even in a domestic abuse situation."

"This is even true with women," Freddie added. "Many people believe women aren't violent and don't hurt each other. One gal had a hunk of her hair ripped out. That's pretty violent."

Burris cringed. "Ouch."

TJ rubbed an index finger against his temple. "Anyway, we

could go on for hours sounding like a public service announcement, but if you come, you'll see for yourself." He lifted Freddie's hand to his lips and dropped a kiss against the knuckles. "But please do as Freddie asked. Try to keep the focus on creating awareness for all domestic violence victims."

Ms. Burris settled her bag's strap over her shoulder. "Sure, let me know when I can come. I'd like to sit in on a few sessions. I might even...well, I might bring a friend along who can benefit."

Freddie pressed a hand against his chest. "Oh, goodness, yes, please do. It's a wonderful group of people. And what's sad is we see new faces every week. I just don't understand where all this violence is coming from." He leaned further into TJ's warm embrace.

Ms. Burris released a long sigh. "I don't know either." She slipped her shoes back on, clacked over, and kissed them both on the cheek. "Text me."

Freddie carried her bag out to the car and watched her pull away. Back inside, he stood in the foyer for a moment, taking a deep breath. That was over. Not as hard as he'd thought it would be, which was likely due to TJ's attendance.

The electric wine bottle opener whirred in the kitchen, and Freddie thought, once again, how well his man knew him. He headed toward the sound. "Ah...perfect, a deep red to soothe my troubled heart. Even though, I've likely had my limit of wine today."

TJ poured a glass of Pinot Noir then handed it over. "Is your heart troubled?"

"No, I'm...relieved. I wasn't sure how it'd go, and I do feel as if I spent too much time talking about us, but...when don't I talk about us?"

TJ grinned, his lips at the edge of his wine glass. "We are awesome."

"Anyway," Freddie took a long draw of the wine, the deep plum notes burst against his palate, and he savored that final hint of spice before he swallowed. He finished off the glass quickly and then took TJ's glass and finished it too. "Yet, I must say, I do feel a little...hollow."

"Hollow?"

"Yeah, I think I need something warm to fill my empty spaces."

"Interesting." TJ tapped a finger against his bottom lip. "Something warm to fill empty spaces, huh?"

After lifting his shirt over his head, Freddie grabbed the wine bottle, and then sashayed back to their bedroom. "I'm sure you can think of a way to solve my problem." He smiled when he heard TJ trailing behind him.

Once in the bedroom, TJ wrapped his arms around Freddie from behind. "I'm proud of you." He dropped kisses along Freddie's neck. "So, I'll I do what I can to fill those empty spaces."

Still with his front to Freddie's back, TJ walked them forward and stopped beside their king-sized bed. He spun Freddie around and took the wine bottle from his hand. After taking a long drink, he handed Freddie the bottle. "Drink."

After they'd finished the wine, TJ's lips had turned a burnished red, and Freddie wanted to taste them more than anything. "I want those red lips on my cock."

TJ pressed a kiss against his forehead before meeting his gaze and winking. "Before we begin, how about we finish getting undressed. After hearing our story, I'm desperate for you." He ran a hand through Freddie's hair. "I could've lost you forever and that's not okay."

Freddie nodded, while unbuttoning his slacks. "Never okay. Now take off your clothes, and then kiss me until I can't breathe."

TJ obliged.

Their mouths melded together, aligning perfectly. Skin

rasping against skin joined with sighs and quiet murmurs, creating their melody. They'd found the perfect rhythm during their time together. A beat that played the perfect song every time

TJ lowered him to the mattress, and then stared down from above, his body braced up on his elbows. "I think you're an amazing man. Sharing your story was very brave."

"Thank you." Freddie ran a finger along TJ's scruffy jawline enjoying the heat that rose on his own face. "But TJ?"

"Yeah?"

"I'm kind of done talking for the day, and I did mention I have an empty space that needs filled so..." He arched his hips, bumping against TJ.

TJ growled and kissed him hard, meshing their mouths together, wet and hot.

Freddie ran his hands up and down TJ's smooth back. "Lube, we need lube. Get it in me now." He squeezed the tip of his dick, sure he was seconds away from shooting all over his stomach.

TJ pressed a hand against Freddie's chest then bent and bit his left nipple, tugging lightly with his teeth.

Freddie braced both feet on the bed and arched up again. "You're gonna make me come from that alone. Fuck, TJ."

"Oh, I like dirty words coming out of that pretty mouth."

"I got dirty words, like all the dirty words."

"Yeah?"

"Yeah. Like get that fat cock in me. Lube up my ass and get the fuck in."

TJ blinked and then rose onto his knees, stroking his leaking cock. "This fat cock?"

Freddie licked his lips. "Okay, lemme taste it first."

"No." TJ flashed a wicked grin, then flipped Freddie over and buried his face in his ass.

The sounds coming out of Freddie's mouth were fit for a porn-movie soundtrack as he begged and screamed for release.

TJ gave no quarter as he went from rimming to fucking him with his tongue to sucking each of his balls and releasing them with a pop.

"Damn you, you know what that sound does to me. Please, baby, please. I need you inside me."

TJ jerked Freddie up to his knees then ran his hands up and down Freddie's back.

He groaned. "God that feels nice."

"You ready for the empty spaces to be filled?"

"Yes, please."

He heard the click of the lube bottle opening, then felt a cool wet finger, circling his tight ring.

TJ opened him with one slick finger, before adding a second.

Freddie loved the slight burn. The fullness. That instant of knowing they'd be joining soon. Becoming one.

"My ass. Mine. No one can take it from me. No one."

"Yes, yours. Show me. Fill me." Freddie glanced over his shoulder and watched as TJ slid a condom over his thick erection.

He grasped Freddie's hips and tugged him into position, nudging his slick hole before pressing past the tight ring.

Freddie relaxed and let him in. "Mmm...yes. So good."

TJ slid in and out a few times, nice and slow before he smacked Freddie's ass and began working in earnest.

The sounds of their bodies slapping together filled the room along with groans and soft pleas.

Freddie gripped the sheets tight.

TJ slowed for a moment and then twisted Freddie's head to the side to deliver a long, wet kiss. He gripped Freddie's erection and stroked in time with both his tongue and cock working inside his body.

Freddie panted into TJ's mouth as his orgasm barreled down his spine. He stiffened and then shouted as he spurted into TJ's working hand.

TJ joined him, his hips stuttering as he came hard inside Freddie's ass.

Thoroughly spent, he hissed as TJ pulled free and then flipped Freddie onto his side.

TJ pulled Freddie's back against his chest and then ran his thumb over Freddie's hole, massaging the muscle.

Freddie jerked as TJ circled the sensitive rim. "You always take good care of me." He dropped his head against TJ's shoulder. "That feels so good, and it's making me want you again."

TJ lifted Freddie's leg over his hip before sheathing himself with a new condom and gently entering him again. On his side, he began the slow slide back and forth. With his free hand, he caressed Freddie's soft dick, bringing it back to life.

Freddie took TJ's hand and licked his jizz covered fingers.

TJ groaned then adjusted his angle a bit, which hit Freddie's sensitive inner spot just right.

Slower this time, TJ rocked against him, hand gliding up and down his chest, with an occasional teasing flick against his cockhead.

Freddie couldn't stop the tears that formed in his eyes. He could've lost this. But they'd survived. "You fill me so good, baby. Don't stop. Make me come again, please. I need it. Need you."

Continuing the slow penetration, TJ came moments later, his hips jerking with each thrust. His groans the most beautiful music against Freddie's ear.

Lost in the sounds of TJ's pleasure, Freddie closed his eyes and gripped his dick. After two strong tugs, he spilled all over his hand.

TJ turned Freddie to face him. "Sex is always perfect with you. Like we've found this rhythm, and we're never out of tune. I love that, you know? It's hot and amazing and beautiful and the only thing I'll ever need."

Freddie grinned and pressed a kiss on TJ's chest right above his thumping heart. "We wrote our own song, didn't we?"

"Think we can play it forever?"

"Yeah, I think we can." Freddie closed his eyes and snuggled against his lover and best friend. Just before he drifted off, he quietly whispered, "We did it, Emily. I took care of him, and he took care of me."

EPILOGUE

A YEAR LATER.

FREDDIE STOOD BESIDE TJ, STARING DOWN AT EMILY's gravestone. The dozen pink roses were a pop of color against the green grass.

He tugged on the collar of his light blue T-shirt. "It's always so muggy in Chicago. Shouldn't it be cooler at this time of night?"

"We lived here most of our lives, Daz. I don't know why you're surprised by the humidity every time we come back here." TJ ran a hand up and down Freddie's back. "We'll head to Mom's in a minute. Wouldn't want you to melt."

"I am sweet enough to melt, yes, but take all the time you need. Emily needs to hear what we've been up to since our last visit."

"Right...yeah." TJ clapped his hands together and then cleared his throat.

"You okay? I know visiting her is still hard."

"I'm fine." TJ smiled and then slipped the backpack he'd

brought along off his shoulder. "Maybe this will keep you from thinking about the heat."

"So, I finally get to see what you secretly packed away in that bag?"

"Yep." TJ pulled a silver soup can from the bag. The label had been removed and holes were poked into the sides.

"Oh." Freddie bounced up and down on his feet. "Are we catching lightning bugs?"

"Yeah." TJ handed over the can. "Knock yourself out."

Freddie took the can and glanced around the cemetery. "There's one. Let's get it." He took a couple steps and tried to swipe the bug into his palm.

TJ laughed when he missed.

"Hey, you try then, mister."

TJ sauntered up beside him, hands cupped together.

"Don't suffocate the poor thing." Freddie pried open TJ's hands then gasped. "Oh my God." His stomach flipped and then some odd scream-squeak erupted from his throat.

Using his index finger, he poked the black gold ring in TJ's palm. Square Amethysts lined the center. It was the most beautiful thing he'd ever seen.

"It needed to be here."

TJ's voice startled him.

"I had to ask you here. In the dark, surrounded by fireflies, and where Emily could see." TJ dropped to one knee.

Freddie took a step back, eyes wide, and his heart beating as loud as a bass drum.

"Freddie Davis, you are my light. My song. My everything. And I hope you'll do me the honor of marrying me. Will you? Marry me?"

Dizzy with an overwhelming love for this man, Freddie fell to his knees and clutched TJ's face between his hands. "Yes," he said the word but no sound came out.

"I'm sorry I didn't hear that?"

"Yes!" Freddie dropped a hard kiss on TJ's lips. "Yes!" Another kiss on his cheek. "Yes. I'll marry you." He kissed TJ's lips again. "This is the most romantic moment ever."

TJ grinned. "It is, yeah."

Freddie shoved his shoulder.

TJ tumbled over but brought Freddie with him. "So you want to marry me?"

"I said, yes."

"I think you need to kiss me to seal the deal."

"I *did* kiss you, but I'll gladly do it again." He leaned down to kiss this amazingly romantic man, but then shot back up. "Wait! Put it on me, please." Freddie wiggled his ring finger. "I don't want you to drop it or something crazy like that, so get it on my finger now!"

"Usually you're telling me to take it off."

"Oh, I'll be saying that later, but right now, get that ring on my finger."

TJ kissed his finger before sliding it on.

Freddie held it up and watched the purple stones twinkle. "It's perfect. Oh, you need one too."

"I do."

Freddie sucked in a breath. "Holy smokes, Hardcastle. You can't say I do yet." He swatted TJ's upper arm. "What's wrong with you? You'll like jinx the whole wedding or something."

TJ kissed his ring finger. "Have I jinxed anything so far?"

"No, you haven't. Do we have to stay here and catch bugs, or can we go back to the hotel and have we-just-got-engaged sex?"

"I'm on board with that, but first, can we take a moment to sit here with Emily. I'd like her to be the first to know that you said, yes."

"Oh, TJ." Freddie sniffed. "Yes, let's tell her."

TJ stood, walked back over to Emily's tombstone, and then settled against it. He held open his arms. "Come here, fiancé."

With a wide smile on his face, Freddie leaned against TJ and together they told Emily everything. The highs, the lows, and before they left, they sang together. A song just for them as the fireflies lit up the sky.

Thank you for reading *Spotlight*. I hope you enjoyed Freddie and TJ's story. If you did, please leave a review at your purchase site. The author appreciates reviews.

Interested in more books by Jillian Jacobs visit:
www.jillianjacobs.com

The National Domestic Violence Hotline: https://www.thehotline.org/is-this-abuse/lgbt-abuse/

Immortal Life of Henrietta Lacks by Rebecca Skloot

ABOUT THE AUTHOR

In the spring of 2013, Jillian Jacobs changed her career path and became a romance writer. After reading for years, she figured writing a romance would be quick and easy. Nope! With the guidance of the Indiana Romance Writers of America chapter, she's learned there are many "rules" to writing a proper romance. Being re-schooled has been an interesting journey, and she hopes the best trails are yet to be traveled.

Jillian is a: Tea Guzzler, Polish Pottery Hoarder, and lover of all things Moose.

The genres she writes under are: Paranormal and Contemporary romance with suspenseful elements.

She is the cofounder of Healing With Words, a not-for-profit that hosts Writers On The River.

Website: www.jillianjacobs.com

www.ingramcontent.com/pod-product-compliance
Lightning Source LLC
Chambersburg PA
CBHW061230170626
46809CB00007B/2602